MW01152514

One You Never Leave

Hades' Spawn Motorcycle Club, Volume 4

Lexy Timms

Published by Dark Shadow Publishing, 2016.

This is a work of fiction. Similarities to real people, places, or events are entirely coincidental.

ONE YOU NEVER LEAVE

First edition. March 4, 2016.

Copyright © 2016 Lexy Timms.

Written by Lexy Timms.

Also by Lexy Timms

Alpha Bad Boy Motorcycle Club Triology
Alpha Biker

Conquering Warrior Series
Ruthless

Diamond in the Rough Anthology
Billionaire Rock
Billionaire Rock - part 2

Dominating PA Series
Her Personal Assistant - Part 1
Her Personal Assistant - Part 2
Her Personal Assistant - Part 3
Her Personal Assistant Box Set

Firehouse Romance Series
Caught in Flames
Burning With Desire
Craving the Heat
Firehouse Romance Complete Collection

Fortune Riders MC Series
Billionaire Biker
Billionaire Ransom
Billionaire Misery

Hades' Spawn Motorcycle Club
One You Can't Forget
One That Got Away

One That Came Back
One You Never Leave
Hades' Spawn MC Complete Series

Heart of the Battle Series
Celtic Viking
Celtic Rune
Celtic Mann
Heart of the Battle Series Box Set

Justice Series
Seeking Justice
Finding Justice
Chasing Justice
Pursuing Justice
Justice - Complete Series

Love You Series
Love Life: Billionaire Dance School Hot Romance
Need Love
My Love

Managing the Bosses Series
The Boss
The Boss Too
Who's the Boss Now
Love the Boss
I Do the Boss
Wife to the Boss
Employed by the Boss
Brother to the Boss
Senior Advisor to the Boss
Forever the Boss
Gift for the Boss - Novella 3.5

Christmas With the Boss

Moment in Time
Highlander's Bride
Victorian Bride
Modern Day Bride
A Royal Bride
Forever the Bride

R&S Rich and Single Series
Alex Reid
Parker

Saving Forever
Saving Forever - Part 1
Saving Forever - Part 2
Saving Forever - Part 3
Saving Forever - Part 4
Saving Forever - Part 5
Saving Forever - Part 6
Saving Forever Part 7
Saving Forever - Part 8

Southern Romance Series
Little Love Affair
Siege of the Heart
Freedom Forever
Soldier's Fortune

Tattooist Series
Confession of a Tattooist
Surrender of a Tattooist
Heart of a Tattooist

Tennessee Romance

Whisky Lullaby
Whisky Melody
Whisky Harmony

The Debt
The Debt: Part 1 - Damn Horse
The Debt: Complete Collection

The University of Gatica Series
The Recruiting Trip
Faster
Higher
Stronger
Dominate
No Rush

T.N.T. Series
Troubled Nate Thomas - Part 1
Troubled Nate Thomas - Part 2
Troubled Nate Thomas

Undercover Series
Perfect For Me
Perfect For You
Perfect For Us

Unknown Identity Series
Unknown
Unexposed
Unpublished

Standalone
Wash
Loving Charity
Summer Lovin'

Christmas Magic: A Romance Anthology
Love & College
Billionaire Heart
First Love
Frisky and Fun Romance Box Collection
Managing the Bosses Box Set #1-3

ONE You Never leave

Hades' Spawn Motorcycle Club Series
Book 4
By
Lexy Timms
Copyright 2016 by Lexy Timms

All rights reserved. No part of this publication may be reproduced, stored in or introduced into a retrieval system, or transmitted, in any form, or by any means (electronic, mechanical, photocopying, recording, or otherwise) without the prior written permission of both the copyright owner and the above publisher of this book.

This is a work of fiction. Names, characters, places, brands, media, and incidents are either the product of the author's imagination or are used fictitiously. Any resemblance to an actual person, living or dead, events, or locales is entirely coincidental. The author acknowledges the trademarked status and trademark owners of various products referenced in this work of fiction, which have been used without permission. The publication/use of these trademarks is not authorized, associated with, or sponsored by the trademark owners.

All rights reserved.
Copyright 2015 by Lexy Timms

Hades' Spawn Motorcycle Club Series

Find Lexy Timms:

Lexy Timms Newsletter:
http://eepurl.com/9i0vD
Lexy Timms Facebook Page:
https://www.facebook.com/SavingForever
Lexy Timms Website:
http://lexytimms.wix.com/savingforever

Description

From Bestselling Author, Lexy Timms, comes a motorcycle club romance that'll make you want to buy a Harley and fall in love all over again.

Emily Dougherty and Luke Wade were in love in high school, but circumstances conspired to keep them apart. Ten years later they meet again and find their connection is just as strong and more searingly hot than ever.

Events take a dangerous turn when Luke's uncle, Mexican drug lord, Raymondo Icherra, shows up and stirs up trouble.

Emily's pregnancy turns high risk with her fainting and having continuous high blood pressure. While Luke deals with a problem with his MC club Hades Spawn, Emily is kidnapped by persons unknown.

As Luke searches frantically for Emily he learns the truth about his past and his parent's murder.

This is book 4 in the Hades' Spawn Series
One You Can't Forget
One That Got Away
One That Came Back
One You Never Leave
One Christmas Night

- *Christmas Novella*

NEW
One Christmas Night
Hades' Spawn Christmas Novella
Now Available!

Luke and Emily have each other, and their toddler son, but every other relationship in their lives is strained—the result of the violent events revolving around the Spawn and the club's president two years before.

When the president of Hades' Spawn, Oakie Walker, insists Luke and Emily host the club's Christmas Party, Luke's not very happy. Though he was reinstated as a member of the Spawn, and maintains their clubhouse, he spends only the time he has to with the club.

Emily's adoptive father, Sam Dougherty, makes no bones that biker Luke is not good enough for his daughter, while her biological father, Rob, wants to get closer to her and his grandson and no one but Emily is happy about it. Add to the mix that the president of a rival motorcycle club, the Rojos, does everything he can to create the impression that Luke will join his gang, and you have a recipe for one explosive Christmas party.

Can Luke and Emily negotiate the tricky currents of the demands from those around them? Or will it damage their relationship if they do?

NEW SERIES Coming January 2017!

EXCERPT INCLUDED!

Making Her His

Saks' Story

Anthony Parks, AKA Saks straddles two worlds and neither one is very reputable. One is as a motorcycle mechanic and Road Captain of the Hades Spawn, a none too squeaky clean motorcycle club. The other is as the scion of an organized crime family who wants him to join the family business, something he is loathed to do.

Recent events with the Spawn has soured his community reputation, and while certain women like bad boys, those kind of women are not who Saks is looking for. Add pressure from his family that "it is time to marry" Saks is faced with an impossible situation.

His wise-guy uncle proposes an arranged marriage between Saks and the daughter of a dom from another crime family. And when he meets a mysterious blonde that shows him love at first sight is possible, he knows that he could never accept his uncle proposal. Now he would just have to figure out a way to tell Uncle Vits without getting excommunicated from the family or putting the Spawn in the crosshairs of a powerful crime organization. While he is doing that he has to find the woman who has stolen his heart.

Christina

Christina Marie Serafini decided a long time ago that her loving but paternalistic family wasn't going to determine the course of her life. She had no desire to get mixed up in any of the many legal and illegal businesses her family owned. Chrissy had earned a Masters in Business and Communications on her own dime, and she just landed her dream job of Director of Marketing for an up and coming business.

Marriage and a family isn't in her game plan right now and when she did marry it was going to be a respectable man. When her grandfather announced he had arranged a marriage for her with "a nice Italian man," Christina goes ballistic. She wasn't going to marry anyone, let alone someone chosen for her. She certainly wouldn't marry a member from another crime family. Chrissy could only imagine what kind of opportunistic carogna would agree to marry a woman he never met.

Urged by her sister to at least check him out, she goes to his family's bar to confirm her suspicions. That's when she finds a handsome biker that knows exactly how to send her emotions and body into overdrive. But realizing the hunky man is the one her grandfather wants to marry sends her into flight mode even though he haunts her dreams.

Once he finds her can Saks convince the woman of his dreams to look past his family connections to take a chance on a lowly motorcycle mechanic? And if he does, can he look past hers?

COMING January 2017

CHAPTER ONE

Business Matters

"Luke," Emily called through the shop. She was louder than she liked, screaming because of the rock music playing in the shop. Emily sat at Luke's desk, going through Luke's books, trying to put some order in the chaotic accounting of her husband. Her aim was to prep for January's tax filing because she knew that after the baby came in January, she'd have little precious time to get things like this done.

Luke didn't answer and she squirmed in the seat. In her seventh month, getting up and down in any seat had become a major operation. She had no idea how she was going to handle the next two months, especially since they were during the holiday season. Already every movement seemed like a major exertion.

"Luke!" she called more loudly.

Luke appeared in the doorway that separated the shop from the office area of Central Valley Bike Repair, wiping his oily hands with a shop rag.

"Yeah, baby?" he said. "Are you okay?" His look of concern was so precious her irritation was forgotten, and she wanted to throw her arms around him right then. As always, she melted when she caught sight of him. His t-shirt accentuated his broad chest and muscled arms, and the sexy scruff he kept on his jaw and chin made her want to nuzzle his neck. Oh, the things that sandpapery scruff did to her when he kissed the back of her neck. Thinking about it, she couldn't wait to get him home. But business first.

"I'm fine; your books are a disaster."

He crossed into the office and to the desk, pulled out the chair, and swiftly kissed her. "That," he said, "is why I married an accountant."

She cocked an eyebrow at him as he leaned over her. He smelled of motor oil, aftershave, and sweat, three things she'd come to associate with him holding her tight and sweeping her into a haze of loving bliss. She cocked an eyebrow at him. "Ulterior motives, I see," she said.

"It doesn't hurt that you're the sexiest accountant ever," he leaned over and breathed into her ear, and she was nearly a goner. Her traitorous body already pooled liquid heat between her legs.

She smacked both of his shoulders with her hands. "What did I say about distracting the accountant?"

"That no good would come of it," he said and chuckled. "And I agree. It's no good not cumming."

"Impossible," she muttered under her breath.

"Hey!" called Saks, sticking his head in the doorway. "Get a room, you two."

"Go back to work," growled Luke, staring steadily at Emily.

"Can't. Work all done."

Luke glanced at the clock and sighed. It was only two o'clock. Emily knew what he was thinking. Winter months were light with work. If it wasn't for the bikes they stored for customers during the long Connecticut winters, Luke would have difficulty making payroll. When Luke was single, he didn't care how his finances flowed. As long he paid his bills, he was good with the financially light winters. But now he had a wife and a baby on the way and, as Emily kept pointing out, every dollar counted.

Maybe she shouldn't keep pointing that out.

"You know, Luke," said Saks. "The offer's still on the table. Lay me off and I can head to Florida until the spring. My dad's got a condo down there. I could use a break from the snow."

"The first flake hasn't even flown yet," mumbled Luke.

"Which makes the offer even more urgent. I don't know about you, but I'm sick of how these winters keep getting worse."

Luke's eyes flicked to Emily and then to Saks. Again, because she was getting to know him so well, she knew what the problem was. Luke didn't want to leave the shop without coverage if something happened to her. Already the baby was bigger than he should be. The obstetrician gave them a list of things to watch for, and Luke kept an eagle eye on her, enough so that he refused to let her get a job of her own, at least for now.

Not that she didn't love spending every minute she could with her gorgeous husband, but she wanted to contribute financially. The least she could do was help with straightening out Luke's books. Already she found Luke overpaid on his federal taxes in the previous year, and she was working on the two years previous to that. At least the money she could recover would help. But she still had a bunch of work to do on those years, and it would take several months for the IRS to go over the amended returns and refund the over-payments.

"Well," said Luke to Saks. "Go ahead and knock off for the day."

"Lay-off?"

"I have to discuss that with the boss here," said Luke, flashing a grin at Emily.

"Okay, I'll give you two some *much needed* time alone." He rolled his eyes as he took his Hades' Spawn jacket from the pegs by the front door. When he opened it, a frigid blast of November air swept through the shop office. "Winter's coming," he growled, hiking the collar up around his neck, and the door shut behind him with a slam.

Luke returned his attentions to Emily. "Alone at last," he said, leaning in to kiss her again. He was barely an inch from her lips when she spoke.

"Um, you, me and the store books. How romantic."

He pulled back. "Ok, Em. Something's got your attention. What is it?"

"Well, these property tax bills of yours. What is this bike here? I don't remember seeing it." She picked up a bill for a bike built in 1980.

Luke studied it a few moments, and Emily could see when the connection clicked.

"That was my first bike. You remember that one? The one I had in high school?"

"You still have it?"

"No. I sold it when I went into the navy."

"Then why are you paying property taxes on it?"

He shrugged. "Didn't know I was."

"Luke Wade!" Emily scolded.

"Look, when I opened the shop I had an accountant who took care of these things. When she quit, I just decided to do things myself. It's the computer age, after all, and the computer program she used was easy enough."

Emily sighed. "And easy enough to repeat her mistakes. Luke, this isn't just a matter of a few hundred misspent dollars. Peach Tree only gets you so far. If something happens with that bike, you're liable."

Luke leaned over again and gave her a kiss on the lips. "I trust you to figure it out and fix it, Em. You've been awesome with all this. How did I ever live without you?"

"Very poorly." She picked at his thread-bare brown t-shirt and tsked. "I'm throwing this out."

"Hey! No way! It'll make a great shop rag!"

"You need some new shirts."

He shrugged and then smiled. "Christmas is coming. You can stock me up on shirts then."

"Oh, Luke," she sighed. Raised in foster homes, Luke never had fabulous Christmases like she and her sister Angela did. The two Dougherty girls would whisper and giggle into the night, getting one stern warning after another from their father to go to sleep, until eventually exhausted, they would. Christmas morning they would fly down the stairs to the living room to find the Christmas tree sparkling with extra glitter strands and piles of boxes underneath. It was magical, the most perfect part of her childhood. This was truer for Emily than her younger sister. Growing up with a sense of disapproval from her parents, especially her father, every Christmas Emily felt there was one person out there, Santa, who cared about her unconditionally.

Of course Santa wasn't real, but the spark of that magical time remained alive in her heart until she did find someone who did love her unconditionally.

She rested her head on Luke's arm. "Let's do this over weekend, or after," she said. "I'm tired, and I just want to curl up in front of the TV with you tonight."

"Wait," Luke said as he poked his head out the doorway and scanned the parking lot for ice that may have formed in the November cold.

"You're being way too overprotective," groused Emily. "I'm fine. I can walk on the blacktop."

He pulled back, gave her a kiss on the cheek, and wound the crook of his arm around hers. Maybe he was overprotective, but there was no way he was going to let anything happen to her, or their baby. The warmth in his heart when he thought of her and his child spread through his body: Their baby; his family. For a kid who grew up without a family of his own, the idea of having a family gripped him in a way that nothing in his life did before. He hadn't had the security of someone who loved and accepted him as he was. And now there was, or would be, two. He couldn't put it in words how he felt, not precise ones anyway, but it was a feeling he treasured each day. When he woke up in the morning with Emily beside him, he couldn't help but be in awe of his luck. When he fell asleep next to her, he looked forward to the next day.

It was a miracle, especially considering that it all could have gone differently. In his senior year of high school, he fell for the slim, blue-eyed blonde, the one with eyes so innocent you'd have thought she was an angel sent from heaven. And she was, at least to Luke; except, her parents hated him, his leather, his bike, and his admittedly wild ways. They forbade her to see him, but she didn't listen. When an eighteen- wheeler forced them off the highway, sending them both sailing over the side of road, Luke suffered enough injuries that he couldn't finish the school year. His disappointment over Emily not visiting was nothing compared to the crush to his heart when he found she went off to college without saying good-bye.

Ten years later, Luke found that Emily lived nearby and sent her a postcard. Lucky for him, she decided to find him, and they started up at the point where they'd left off. They loved each other, enough to weather her parents' disapproval, the interference of an abusive ex-boyfriend, and the DEA taking over his life because of his club's leadership in drug-dealing. It could have gone badly, and indeed seemed like it did, especially the last day of that mess when a rival biker gang forced a showdown at the Hades' Spawn clubhouse at the back of the Luke's property. Bullets flew that day, and he and Emily were lucky to have walked away with their lives.

It was a miracle, and he pulled her closer to him. He wasn't going to lose her again.

Emily held onto his arm despite a little roll of her eyes, and came with him out of the shop. He locked the door and set the security codes as she held on, nuzzling the side of his neck. This distracted him enough that he was startled when he heard the crunch of a footstep on the sand that he had put out on slick spots.

Both he and Emily turned their heads at the same time. Luke frowned at the familiar figure that stood ten feet away from them.

The man in the beige raincoat glared at him.

"What do you want, Anglotti?" growled Luke.

"Luke," said Emily softly.

"No," snapped Luke. "This guy's caused us enough trouble." The memory of Luke's apartment thrown into disarray by this man and his buddies flashed in Luke's mind.

"I'm not here on official business," said the detective.

"Emily," said Luke, handing her the car keys, "go warm up the SUV for me."

"Okay, Luke," said Emily, biting her lip. She took the keys and trudged to the truck.

Luke crossed his arms. "So, what do you want?" he said stiffly.

"The last time your uncle's men entered the country, we escorted them to the airport."

"Yeah," said Luke. "I know."

"This time, they want a sit-down. My boss is taking it."

An icy feeling spread through Luke. "What the hell does that mean?"

"It can only be about you, because we don't want anything to do with Mexican drug dealers; just thought you should know." Anglotti turned away, and then looked at Luke over his shoulder. "Merry Christmas," he sneered.

Luke glared at the asshole cop and watched him get into his car. *Like I don't have enough on my plate!* He stomped over to his SUV and hopped in.

"That handsome face is too drawn and pinched," Emily teased and then frowned. "Something wrong, baby?"

He put the truck in gear to back up. "Nothing," he said flatly.

Emily put her hand on his arm. "Luke," she said gently. "I know you better than that. What did Detective Anglotti want?"

"He wanted to wish us a Merry Christmas."

Emily sighed. When Luke got this way, withdrawn and hard-headed, there was little she could do to change his mood. It annoyed her when he drew that mask of impenetrability up but she bit back the churlish answer she was ready to spit. It was Luke's childhood that had drummed that protective facade into him. His foster home experience left him feeling like it was him against the world. Whatever Anglotti said to him must have stirred up those thoughts.

She understood this. The events of the past few months proved to Luke just how up against the world he was. Luke had two government agencies on his back, the president of his motorcycle club, Hades' Spawn, and two gangs, the one-percenter motorcycle club, the Rojos, and their affiliated street gang, the Hombres. It was a miracle that they got out from under that mess with their lives.

There were still problems that came out of all of it. Because Luke's parents had entered the country illegally, the only legal papers he had were the ones WITSEC gave him. He got those when his father entered the program to testify against his brother's Mexican drug cartel. The DEA used the threat of deportation to push Luke into being their informant on Jack Kinney's activities. Yet now that the operation was over, and Kinney and his cohorts sat in jail awaiting trial, the DEA seemed to have lost their motivation to help Luke. Except for the K-1 visa, which they got so Luke could stay to testify, they didn't live up to their promise of securing proper legal papers for him. There were always delays, and more vague reassurances that everything would be all right once Luke testified. But who knew when those cases would get to court?

Getting married proved more of a chore than it needed to be because of legal paper situation. They had to secure his Mexican birth certificate to get married under his birth name, Raymondo Icherra. It was a point of law that galled Luke, but Luke's attorney, Matt Stone, assured him that once his citizenship came through, Luke was free to change his name. Right now, Luke was living in the country he grew up in under a K-1 visa and there was a whole lot of back and forth to get that. After that, he needed a new driver's license with his legal name on it, and a new social security card. When Emily thought about all the tense moments to get all this straightened out, she got a headache. It was a real mess, but finally they had received the temporary visa and the marriage license.

Maybe a good dinner, and then some snuggling under a blanket while watching a movie would put him in a better mood. Certainly, not cooking would put her in a better mood. "How about pizza tonight?" she suggested.

"Pizza?" said Luke with suspicion. "I thought we were watching our pennies, Mrs. Wade."

She didn't bother to correct him that legally she was Mrs. Icherra. The point would only bring up an argument not worth having. Plus, she'd gone and had to have the name changed to Wade. "I think we can spring for a pizza and just maybe a six-pack."

"Wow, pulling out all the stops, aren't you? What's the occasion?"

"I just want to see the man I love happy."

"Oh really?"

"Mamma's not happy unless Daddy's happy."

He glanced at her slyly. "You know what's going to make Daddy happy?"

She giggled. "Oh, I've already got that department covered. Food first, then dessert."

His grin widened into a smile. "That's what I like to hear."

CHAPTER TWO

Complications

"Oh, for fuck's sake!" Luke slammed the door when he came back from the mail kiosk.

Emily stood in the kitchen, getting the plates for dinner, and nearly dropped them on the floor when Luke exploded. Her husband might swear, but she hardly ever heard him drop the F-bomb. Nor did he slam the door. "What is it, baby?"

"The fucking USCIS! They sent a letter saying that they are going to do random home inspections to make sure we are living together as a married couple!"

"What?" If Luke wasn't so distressed, Emily would have laughed at the ludicrous situation. She walked to Luke in the living room and took the letter from his hand. "Baby, it isn't a big deal," she said, gently kissing his cheek. "So they come. Big deal. What're they going to find? That you have stinky feet? That I can barely get out of bed without your help? That your wife is about to pop? That's a pretty good clue we *are* married, and with a healthy sexy life."

Luke ran his hand over the top of his close-shaved head. "It's just one more thing to deal with."

She rubbed his jaw with her hand. Many women didn't like the feel of a man's five o'clock shadow, but she loved it. "Babe, it's going to be okay. Really." She smiled at him.

Just then the doorbell rang.

"There, that's the pizza. Go get it and I'll grab you a beer."

Luke sighed, and looked over his shoulder. "Stinky feet?" he glowered.

"Yep. You know it. That's another thing you need, a new pair of boots. And a whole lotta socks."

Luke groaned.

Emily just smiled at him. She was keeping a list of these things in her head. The Everything-He-Needed list was a growing one, but she knew Luke had other concerns, number one being finding a bigger place for them to live. They had moved into his apartment because it was larger than her old one, but the one-bedroom apartment was not big enough for their growing family. Plus, there was a whole host of baby things and furniture they needed. She knew that not for a second did he regret that she was pregnant with their child, but sometimes thinking about their expanding responsibilities unsettled him.

And the USCIS wanted to check if they were really married. What a joke!

Luke opened the door and frowned when he didn't see the pizza delivery man. Emily stood behind to see who was there.

Instead, a very thin woman in a gray wool coat stood at the door. Her dark hair was piled into a bun and her face had the pinched look of someone overworked. "I'm looking for Mr. and Mrs. Icherra."

"What? Oh, that's me. And the wife, of course."

"The name on the mailbox says Wade."

"Well, that was my name before the government took it away."

The woman frowned and looked through some papers in her hand.

"Luke, who is it?" Emily came to the door. She glanced at the woman and smiled. "Hello," she said holding out her hand, "I'm Emily."

The woman looked up. "I'm Agent Coates from the USCIS. I'd like to ask you some questions."

"Really?" She shook the surprise from her face. "Please come in, Agent Coates. We were expecting pizza delivery." Emily ushered the woman into their home and settled her in the chair that sat kitty-corner to the couch.

Luke sank onto the sofa and Emily sat next to him and took his hand.

"What can we do for you, Agent?" asked Emily.

"I have some questions about your application."

"My application?" said Luke. "We went through all that in our interview."

"Well, there are irregularities in your application. You did enter the country illegally."

"Yes, that's true. My parents brought me in when I was five."

"And you didn't apply through the U.S. consulate in your country."

"Begging your pardon, but *this* is my country, Agent. I can't help it if my parents brought me here when I was too young to know the difference."

"Not according to the law, Mr. Icherra," she replied sharply.

Luke took out his cell phone. "Maybe we should get my lawyer in on the conversation."

"That won't be necessary," said Coates.

"Maybe it is. You're talking about matters of law and it's my lawyer who has been handling my case. I admit my case is mess— unique. Somehow, and now I don't even know how with everything we went through, WITSEC got my father, my mother, and me into government witness protection. All my identification papers came out of their program. As far as I knew, I was an American citizen. I went to public school, served in the U. S. Navy for heaven's sake, and went to college here. Now, because of the screwed up paperwork of one government agency, I'm in trouble with another one."

The woman set her jaw and looked down at her papers. "And despite this, you marry an American citizen. It seems a bit too convenient."

"Is that so?" said Luke tersely.

"When did you meet Emily?"

"In high school. We dated."

"Is that right, Mrs. Icherra?"

"Actually, my name is Wade. When we married, I changed my name to Wade so that when Luke did become a citizen we wouldn't have to change two names. It's all perfectly legal. Our lawyer assured us of that."

"I see," said Coates, as if she didn't. "And you met in high school?"

"Yes. We were both seventeen."

"I see. So you were apart for an extended period."

"Ten years," said Luke.

"And how did you reunite?"

"It was the sweetest thing," said Emily. "He sent me a postcard telling me he'd never stopped thinking about me. It was one of the promotional postcards from his motorcycle shop,"

"One of the old ones, from the previous owner," said Luke.

"That's right," said Emily brightly, "and I tracked him down."

Luke chuckled at that.

"And when did all this happen?"

"The spring," said Emily.

"We've been together ever since," said Luke.

"Well," said Emily, "except for the summer. Luke was pushed into being an informant for the DEA and he didn't want me in danger, so he pretended he didn't want me."

"I see," said Coates even more tersely. "The DEA. Why?"

"The old president of my motorcycle club was dealing drugs, but they couldn't get anything on him."

"And were you involved in his activities?"

"No! I just did what the DEA wanted: kept an eye on him and reported everything."

"Uh-huh," said the agent as if she didn't believe him. "You realize that involvement with drug activities immediately disqualifies you for a visa to remain in this country."

"Look!" said Luke sharply. "I was threatened with deportation if I didn't cooperate with the DEA. You can't hold me accountable for that. I kept as far away from Kinney and his shit as I could."

"Luke," chided Emily softly. "Agent Coates, perhaps you should speak with DEA Agent Leo Moyes. He was the agent in charge of the case. He'll confirm that Luke is required to stay in the country to testify in the case."

"That may be so, but from what I see here I don't see how Mr. Icherra can remain in the country. He was here illegally for longer than six months, and that usually requires that he has to leave and stay out of the country for ten years before he can apply for a visa to return."

Luke glared at the agent and Emily put her hand on his arm. "That's why we have a lawyer, Agent Coates," said Emily softly. "We're aware of the difficulties of Luke's unusual case."

"Oh, I see more than difficulties. The short time you were together before you married is a big red flag. Association with criminal elements is another. Being here illegally is yet another. Your unusual application process... the list seems to go on, doesn't it?"

"Well," said Luke, "as my wife said, that's why we have a lawyer."

Agent Coates stood. "We'll be in touch. I'll need to look into this. It requires a lot more investigation. I would suggest not going anywhere. Don't try hiding in another state."

"My wife's about to have a baby! This is bull—"

"Thank you for coming by," Emily cut him off and shepherded the woman to the door. When she clicked the door shut, she shook her head at him.

Luke swore again. "Did you have to be so fucking nice to her?"

"Really? This is my fault?"

Luke opened his mouth to argue and then closed it again.

"It doesn't do any good to be rude to a federal agent. She's just doing her job."

"Yeah," said Luke, "like Moyes and Hector were doing their jobs."

Emily bit her lip. Leo Moyes pressured Luke into becoming an informant. But it was Hector Garcia, the DEA agent, who pretended to be Luke's loyal friend. That galled her husband the most. "Sit; I'll bring you a beer."

"You've said that before woman, and I'm still waiting."

"Well, if you're complaining, get your own beer." She walked away and Luke caught her arm and pulled her back, twirling her so that her side pressed against his body. Emily threw her arms around his neck as he put his hand on her rounded belly. The baby kicked just then, which brought a smile to Luke's face.

"Little guy is getting big," said Luke huskily.

"Don't I know it," sighed Emily. "I'll be glad when the baby is born and I don't feel like I have a basketball for a stomach."

Luke rubbed little circles where the baby kicked. "I like your stomach. It's sexy."

"No, it is not!" she said.

He nibbled the back of her neck and she shivered. "You don't get to say what I find sexy. You can think what you want about your stomach, but to me it means you are growing our child inside you, and that's hot."

She leaned against him, loving his husky voice so close to her ear saying such sweet things to her.

"I love you," she sighed.

"Same here." He raised his hand to her breasts and rubbed her nipple, which had pebbled and stuck out from her bra. "I love how full your breasts are now, and how sensitive they are to my touch."

Liquid heat gathered between Emily's legs as his fingers played with her nipples through her shirt. It was true that after the first rough months of her pregnancy her body became incredibly sensitive to Luke's caresses.

"I bet," he said in low voice, "if I felt between your legs, I'd find how wet you are."

Emily swallowed. It was true that Luke made her crazy with desire every time he touched her. Being pregnant amplified her physical need for him. Luke took Emily's tiny hand and placed it on his crotch, where she found the swell of his arousal through his jeans. She stroked the steely length through the fabric, and he sighed. "Woman, what you do to me."

"The pizza's going to be here any moment," said Emily.

"I don't have either pizza or beer in my hand at the moment, and I need to put my mouth on something."

In a second, Luke jerked up her shirt over her head and unsnapped her bra, letting her creamy white breasts spill out. Luke leaned in and sucked up a nipple sharply and hard, causing Emily to arch backward with a sharp hiss. He let that one drop and took the other one, suctioning it just as tightly and swirling his tongue around the tender nub.

"Please, Luke," she pleaded.

"I'd like to please you," he said, lifting his head briefly from her creamy orbs.

"Baby," she pleaded again.

His hands wandered to her cleft. His fervent attention to her nipples and her anticipation of his touch on her rapidly-swelling clit ramped up her desire. Her panties were soaked with her slickness, and the delicious fire of arousal spread through her body. Her husband leaned into her thigh again, pressing his hard, jean-clad length into her.

"See what you do to me, baby," he whispered in her ear. She shivered and bent her face towards his lips. He took her lips swiftly, slipping his tongue inside her mouth and caressing her own with it. Luke tasted like he always did, hot and masculine, the warmth of his kiss overpowering her resistance.

"The pizza'll be here any minute," she said weakly.

"Then we'll have to be quick," he said with a wicked smile. "Grab the top of the sofa, and bend over!"

"What?"

He gave her a light slap on her bottom. "You heard me."

Emily giggled at the wicked image of her husband taking her with her bent over the sofa. But she liked the thought too, so she did as Luke ordered.

Luke jerked down her work-out pants that she donned for comfort, and her panties, and quite unexpectedly dropped to his knees and pressed his tongue upward between her legs, lapping up the juices that pooled there. His tongue laved her most sensitive places, sending jolts of electricity through her. She moaned and was rewarded by Luke thrusting up even harder, the scruff from his five o'clock shadow scraping her thighs in the most delicious way. It wasn't painful, but it made her even more aware of the ministrations Luke lavished on her clit and folds. His tongue curled and caressed the soft flesh of her labia and hood, and she came in a rush, crying his name and bucking against his face.

When she calmed, he rose and bent over to wickedly descend on her mouth with a crushing kiss so she tasted her own juices. "See now hot you taste," he said. "I could eat that all night, you taste so good."

She swallowed hard at the thought. Emily was so sensitive after her orgasm she doubted she could take any more of Luke's tongue's attention.

"But," he said with a gleam in his eye, "it's my turn now. Hold on tight, baby."

Emily gasped as she felt him lining up his hard shaft to her entrance. She was so wet both from his mouth and her orgasm that he slid in easily. He groaned as his length moved deeper inside her. He filled her completely and gripped her hips. Emily couldn't help but mewl; he felt so good inside her. "I love you, baby," she gasped.

"Hell, yeah," Luke was like this when he was deep in pleasure, unable to speak more than a word or two.

"So good," she whimpered.

Slowly he pumped her, his strong thighs pushing into her and then out. Slowly his rhythm built. In her mind, she saw him from the back, his beautiful ass tight and strong as he stroked her. The image was enough to tip her over the edge again. Her cries aroused him more, and he pounded into her.

"Fuck!" he said, "I'm cumming, baby." After a few more strokes, he laid his head on her back for a minute while his breathing calmed. Then he straightened and pulled her up into his arms.

"You are so amazing," she said and smiled. "That was quick. The pizza isn't even here yet."

"Oh, yeah, that. I told them to hold delivery for an hour."

"You!" accused Emily, slapping her hand on his shoulder.

"Ouch!" he said.

"Don't even go there. With muscles like yours, this isn't even the sting of a mosquito bite on you."

"But," said Luke, playfully with a touch of drama, "the emotional pain."

Emily scoffed, but the sound was overridden by the ring of the doorbell.

CHAPTER THREE

Ignoring Good Advice

Luke let go of Emily as the doorbell chirped. She made her way to the bedroom to get herself together while Luke hastily flung his clothes back on. He managed to get his pants back up as the doorbell rang again, and he slipped his t-shirt on as he answered the door to find a tall dark-haired man.

"Matt!" said Luke surprised.

"Hey, I hope I didn't come at a bad time, but I thought if the immigration agent was still here it might help to have your lawyer around as well."

"No, she left a half hour ago. But come in anyway and have a beer."

"Sounds good."

"Emily, Matt Stone's here."

Emily came out of the bedroom after pulling on a pair of pregnancy jeans and a t-shirt. Her face was flushed and Luke grinned at how sexy she looked. "Hi, Matt; I didn't know lawyers made house calls."

"You're looking great, Emily," said Matt.

"Nah. I'm a whale and I know it. But at least it's not a permanent condition."

"Em!" Luke said laughing. "You're tiny! You just think you're big." He walked over and kissed her. "You look gorgeous." He nodded at the sofa. "Sit and I'll get you something to drink. Matt, have a seat too. We've got a pizza due here any minute."

"I don't want to impose."

"Not at all!" Emily patted Matt's arm and pointed to the recliner. "You come to an Irish woman's house and you'll get fed.

If you don't eat, it's your own damn fault. At least that's what my mother always said."

Matt grinned widely. "I swear if you weren't taken, I'd take you off the market myself."

"Hey, stop flirting with my wife," complained Luke with a crooked smile.

"Got to keep the skills up somehow. I'm too buried in the office for much of a social life. You're too damned lucky, Luke." Matt winked at Emily and she chuckled.

The doorbell chimed again.

"That better be the pizza," Luke joked. In short order, he brought two boxes to the coffee table. "Sausage and peppers, and a white pizza," he said, pointing to the boxes.

"White pizza?" said Matt.

"It's yummy," said Emily. "Lots of garlic and parmesan cheese."

Matt shrugged off his charcoal gray suit jacket and laid it across the wide back of the upholstered chair. With a smile, he lifted the cover of one of the boxes. "Well, if it's from Jimmy's, it's got to be good."

Luke brought over a couple of beers and handed one to Matt. He handed a lemonade to Emily, and dumped paper plates and napkins on the coffee table. "It's been a day, so we're casual tonight."

"I didn't expect dinner, so this is a treat."

Luke sank down in the sofa next to Emily and popped the cap off of his beer. He waited till Matt had his pizza. "So that agent had some pretty dire things to say about my case."

"They aren't known," said Matt, "for their warm and caring personalities. They like to scare people, usually to try to get them say things that will count against the immigrant."

Luke scowled. "Funny. I don't feel like an immigrant."

"Your father did you no favors for doing things like he did. That counts against you. But the government is not living up to their old promises, which should work for you."

"Will it?" said Emily.

"I won't lie to you, Emily. Luke's case is unusual, and immigration doesn't like unusual. If the DEA doesn't step up for Luke, he may have to go to Mexico. There are some nice cities, and I hear Hermisillo is a lot like Tucson."

"I have no interest in living in Mexico," said Luke. "I'd rather go to Canada."

"Wouldn't we all," said Matt with a chuckle. He tipped back his beer and took a long sip.

"Well," said Emily, "I don't want to go to either place. When I was in California, a few friends and I went to Mexico for spring break. I'm not eager to repeat *that* experience. And Canada? I would miss my mother and sister and our friends. Luke would miss his brothers in Hades' Spawn. Moving is not a good solution."

"Canada's not an option without papers either." Stone nodded his head, but Luke could see the wheels turning in the lawyer's mind. They might not have any choice about the matter. "You should both try to get passports just in case. Luke, you'll need to go the Mexican consulate, but Emily you can just go to any U. S. Post Office. It'll be easier to move around, should Luke get deported, if you have your passports. Luke, you could possibly go to another country if you don't want to stay in Mexico, and Emily, you'll be able to follow Luke."

Emily sighed, and Luke put his arm around her.

"Don't worry, baby. I'm sure it won't come to that."

"But it seems to me," said Emily, "that Luke's immigration status here will cause the same problems to get a Mexican passport as it is for him to get a resident visa here in the United States."

"Can't pull anything over on you, Emily. But it doesn't hurt to try."

"Matt, take a look at that for me legally. I agree that getting the passport is a good idea. The last thing I want is being stuck in Mexico close to my uncle. It's just not healthy." Or safe. Not for him, or Emily and the baby.

"Okay, Luke," agreed Matt. "I can see I'm going to earn that bike."

"Bike?" said Emily with suspicion in her voice. "What bike?"

Luke grimaced. "I thought you didn't tell your client's secrets," accused Luke.

"She's your wife. I thought she knew."

"What's going on?"

"Nothing, Emily. We're just doing a bit of horse trading. I promised the 883 to him when the work was finished."

"But you love that bike!" she protested.

"I love all my bikes, sweetheart, but I love you more. I'll do anything to stay with you. And I don't need three bikes anyway. With you in my life, I'm less likely to ride it."

Emily bit her lip, her face drawn up in consternation.

"Really, babe," said Luke. "Don't think another thing about it. It's all good." It wasn't like his bike was going to have a bucket seat attached with Emily riding along beside him. It was time to man up.

Emily blew out a breath. "Okay. We'll talk about it later. Boys, if you don't mind, I'm feeling a bit tired. I'm going to lie down a bit."

"Sure, Emily. Good to see you." Matt stood and shook her hand.

"You okay?" asked Luke, his concern spiking for his wife.

"Yeah. Like you said, it was a day." She gave him a little smile. "For some reason I'm all worn out." She touched his shoulder as she walked around the end of the sofa, and he raised his hand to hers and touched it briefly before she walked away. Emily left the room and clicked the bedroom door shut.

"You want another beer, Matt?"

"No, I'm good. Driving, you know? The last thing a judge wants to see is a lawyer in his courtroom with a DUI."

Luke got himself another beer, and returned to see Matt staring at his beer bottle with a very serious expression.

"Something up?" said Luke.

"Yeah. I got Okie his new trial."

"Really? That's great." Okie was Doug Black's club handle and president-in-absentia of the Hades' Spawn MC club. Luke was supposedly running things until Okie was released.

"Is it, Luke? Isn't the last thing you need a known associate who was put in jail for dealing drugs? It's bad enough that Gibs was arrested for drug possession, and he was your employee."

"All that was engineered by Jack Kinney," spit Luke.

"Yeah, but there was truth in some of it, wasn't there? At least with Gibs."

Luke looked away, his eyes narrowing. He didn't like to talk ill of the dead. "He was carrying the heroin," said Luke quietly. "Gibs should've known better."

"Whatever the circumstance, that club is poison to you, Luke. I think you have to think over everything and make some decisions here. As your lawyer, I'm advising you to disavow Hades' Spawn and resign the vice-presidency. Distance yourself before more bullshit goes down with them and spoils your chance for citizenship irreparably."

Luke closed his eyes, trying to contain his anger. True, Jack Kinney fucked things up by bringing in the Tucson crew and trying to muscle into the drug trade of the Hombres, one of the largest street gangs in Connecticut. But things were straightened out now. Kinney and his crew were in jail awaiting trial, the old members Kinney scared off came back, and their president was about to return. Now Stone wanted him to give them up after everything he did to get things straight!

Gibs died. He couldn't dishonor that or the man by turning his back on his club. "No," said Luke through clenched teeth.

"What's more important to you, Luke? A motorcycle gang, or your wife and child and the life you can have here?"

"The Spawn *is* part of my life!"

Matt shook his head. "Your decision, Luke. But do me a favor and think about it. Think about what's important." Matt sighed and stood. "Thanks for dinner," he said as he put on his suit jacket. "I'll be in touch."

Luke saw Matt out the door while the words the man spoke rolled in his gut. His head told him the lawyer was right, but his heart argued furiously otherwise. The Spawn were the people who'd kept him together after he returned alone from the navy. Their business helped him to morph from doing a few repairs on the side into a thriving business. His life during riding season revolved around the club events, and he'd even built a clubhouse that did a good business through the riding season. Giving up the Spawn would be giving up a good part of his life.

But what about Emily and the baby? his head spoke urgently. *Do you really want to risk them?*

No. No. A thousand times, no. He'd lost her twice. Luke wasn't going to lose her again. Luke kicked the door. Even through his work boots, pain shot up through his big toe. "Ouch!"

"Luke," called Emily, "everything okay?"

"Yeah. I just stubbed my toe."

"But you're wearing your work boots."

"Yeah, about that. I'm going to take them off now, so you'd better stuff cotton up your nose. You know, so you don't suffer the effects of my stinky feet."

"Come here, you silly man," she said with a laugh.

"I thought you were sleeping."

"Nope. Just resting. There's a difference between resting and sleeping."

"Uh-huh," said Luke as he entered the bedroom. He sat on the edge of the bed and pulled his left foot across his knee to get at the laces of his work boots.

"Why did you promise to give Matt one of your bikes?"

Luke shrugged. "Lawyers aren't cheap, Emily. I'd rather part with the bike than the money."

"Luke, is there something you're not telling me about our finances?"

"Me? You're the accountant. You have access to everything." At that, Luke felt a pang of guilt. He hadn't told her about the money his father had taken and hidden from the Icherra drug cartel. Twelve point five million dollars would go a long way to easing their money troubles. But the last thing he wanted to do was take that money and use it. Luke always felt a sense of pride that he hadn't fallen back on that dirty money, but made his own. No. That money would be for emergencies.

His phone on the nightstand rang and Emily reached over and answered.

"Okay, thanks for letting us know." She clicked off the call. "You might not want to pull that boot off. That was the security company. The store's alarm went off."

Luke groaned. "Probably another coyote sniffing around the fire pit where we roasted that pig last summer."

"The police are there now and they didn't see anything."

"Well, that's what the alarm is for—to scare off the man or beast that's trespassing. But I'm not looking forward to another face to face with Westfield's finest."

"You've got to turn off the alarm, so you can't avoid it."

He finished retying his laces and gave her a kiss on the forehead. "I'll be back in a few minutes. No man or beast is going to keep me from my beautiful Emily for long."

Luke's truck moved through the chilly November night. It didn't take him too long to make it to the shop. In fact, his heat had barely kicked on before he reached the parking lot. He squinted against the flashing lights of the police car parked at the shop's entrance.

"Hello, officers," he said as he walked to the door. He didn't recognize either one of the cops.

"You the owner?" asked one.

"Yes. Luke Wade."

"This is second alarm this month. One more and we're going to have to charge you for coming out."

"Well, I'll try to avoid having coyotes wander over my property."

"No reports of coyotes tonight," said the other office, a baby-faced man who looked like he wasn't two seconds out of the academy.

"When you get that alarm off, we'll walk the property with you," said the other.

Luke flipped up the hinged cover and punched in the code, and the alarm fell silent.

"Check the front," the older officer said to his partner, and they both pulled their flashlights off their thick uniform belts. "Mr. Wade, please come along with me to see if anything is out of place. What's in the back?"

"The entrance to the garage for the bikes we store, and our clubhouse."

"Clubhouse?"

"Yes, for the Hades' Spawn."

"Hmph," said the officer, whose tag said Rawlings. "Any reason anyone is there now?"

"No. Closed up for the winter. The last time I used it was last month for my wedding reception. I'll reopen it in the spring."

"Wedding, eh? Well, let's check it. Maybe a homeless person thought it was a good place to bunk."

That was possible. Luke had put in some mini-apartments, looking to rent them, but that plan didn't work out; not since a deadly shootout had taken place there.

The floodlight for the back switched on as the motion sensor caught Luke moving in to the back parking lot. He checked in the windows of the garage as the officer swung his flashlight in; everything seemed fine. He walked to the front door of the clubhouse, and it was secure. "There's a door in the back," Luke said.

"Any floodlight there?"

"No."

"Then walk behind me."

Rawlings walked swiftly toward the back of the clubhouse; the gravel at the side of the building crunched under his feet. Luke didn't move as fast and soon lost sight of him in the nighttime gloom.

"Stop! Police!" Luke heard. He doubled his steps and almost collided with the police officer.

"Sorry, Mr. Wade. Whoever it was got away before I could chase him. But it looks like the lock's broken here."

Luke inspected the lock and shook his head. Sometimes the things people did amazed him. "You mean the guy heard the alarm and stuck around anyway? Isn't that weird?"

"Yeah, it is. But since you did have a trespasser, this call won't count against you for a false alarm. You might want to think about getting a guard dog to patrol the area."

"Thanks for the idea," said Luke. But he seriously doubted he was going to get a dog to hang around the shop.

"Do you have something to board up this door?" said the officer

That wasn't going to help Luke much, as the building and the door were metal. He went inside the clubhouse, pushed as many tables and chairs from the bar area as he could against the door to hold it shut, and exited by the front door. By the time he was done, the police were gone. A creepy feeling of someone watching washed through him when he climbed into his truck to go home. He shook it off and blamed it on the events of the night.

CHAPTER FOUR

Emily's Encounter

The next day, Luke sat at the desk across from Emily, on the phone with Matt Stone. He mentioned nothing to Emily about the night before except to say that the alarm had been a false one. He had no intention of worrying his wife or putting any unneeded stress on her. It had just been a one-off, so there was no need to worry. "Thanks, Matt. That's great news." His voice didn't sound cheerful and he could see Emily's eyebrows press together as he hung up the phone.

"What did he say?" Emily played with a paperclip on the corner of the papers she was holding.

"That we can get the Mexican passport application online, and send it to the Mexican consulate with the application fee."

Emily nodded. "Okay, I'll get it off the Internet and print it. Here," she said, holding up the result of her morning's work. "Sign this."

Luke looked over the form his wife handed him. "What is it?"

"It's a request to the DMV to send you a copy of the change of title for the bike you sold all those years ago. We need that to get so we can get the taxes taken off your tax bill."

"Really? We have to go through all that?"

"Yes. And some other paperwork, too, that I still need to dig up. I suppose you don't have a copy of the receipt for the plates you turned in or the bill of sale?"

"I don't remember if I turned in the plates, and I just took cash for the bike. I was busy getting inducted into the navy."

Emily suppressed a sigh. The young Luke she remembered wasn't that responsible – apparently with his paperwork or his possessions – and it was causing problems now. "Okay, we'll deal with one item of proof at a time."

He grinned and winked at her. "It was a nice bike, though; a 1977 sportster Ironhead. I bought it after my other bike got trashed. That's when I fell in love with sportsters. Boy, could that bike move."

"Uh-huh," said Emily. "Well, you have three other bikes we're paying taxes on, baby, which are coming up next January. I'd like this one off our list." She patted her belly. "And add this little sportster to your list."

He kissed her cheek indulgently. "My little accountant."

"Who loves you very much." She bent down and picked up the sales from the week. "I'm going to take this cash to the bank."

"You want me to go with you?"

"Nah, it's not that much. I'm just going to the drive-up window. After that I'll go home and put my feet up."

Luke winced when she said "It's not that much" and mentally kicked himself. Emily didn't mean it as offensive. He looked down at her feet, which were beginning to swell from sitting for a long stretch, and grimaced. He knew as well as she did that the swelling feet were not a good sign. "When are you going to see the doctor again?"

"In a couple weeks."

Luke helped her with her coat, and wrapped her scarf around her neck. "I want you to call and make an appointment sooner. Your blood pressure should be checked."

"Such a mother hen," she laughed.

"Better a mother hen than...," he stopped, not willing to voice his thoughts. The doctor told both of them about the dangers of pre-eclampsia, a condition where the mother's blood pressure soars dangerously high, leaving the mother at risk of stroke or worse.

"It's okay, Luke. I feel fine."

"You know darn well that's no assurance against pre-eclampsia. No more pizza for you," he scolded. "And no more restaurant food. We've been playing fast and loose with salt restrictions and that's going to stop."

Emily rolled her eyes. "Yes, sir; now let me get to the bank."

"Okay," he said. "Be careful."

"Luke," she protested.

"Baby. I lost you twice. I'm not going to lose you again." He told her that all the time but there was no way he was letting her go from him ever again. No matter what.

"Don't worry," she said. "There's not a chance in the world I'm letting you out of my sight ever again."

Emily made it to the bank and then realized they didn't have anything for dinner. She wanted to make sure there was something on the stove before Luke came home. Otherwise he'd insist on cooking, and the resulting mess would be more work than if she did it herself. Something made in the slow-cooker could work. Maybe stew. That was easy enough.

She walked into the grocery store and was immediately drawn to the Thanksgiving flower displays. Done in greens with white, yellow, and orange carnations, the table decorations were cheery and bright. Still, seeing the twenty-five-dollar price tag, Emily couldn't bring herself to purchase one. Every dollar counted, and this was a frivolity they couldn't afford.

"Pretty, aren't they?" said a masculine voice with a Hispanic accent behind her.

"Yes," said Emily, looking over her shoulder. An elderly man, about her height with salt and pepper hair and brown skin like he spent time in sun, stood next to her.

"You should get one."

"Not this time," she said.

"Why not?"

She shrugged her shoulders. "I'm just here to get dinner."

"That's nice. Women nowadays don't seem interested in cooking."

She smiled. "Well, my mother always cooked, so I suppose I come by it naturally."

"I'm sure your husband appreciates it."

"I suppose," said Emily. The man seemed unnaturally interested in her, and his close proximity to her made her feel creeped out. People tended to invade her space bubble these days because of her belly. She still hadn't gotten used to strangers coming up and wanting to put their hands on her belly. She hated it, actually.

"When's your baby due?"

It was a question Emily got often when she was in public, but this man who'd come out of nowhere definitely left her feeling unsettled. She wanted to just go home. It was silly, but she just wanted to be anywhere but here. "Listen, I have to go. Nice talking to you."

The man grabbed her arm. "Emily, please don't go."

She jerked her arm up to dislodge his hand. "How do you know my name? I don't know you."

"But I know you, Emily. You're Raymondo's wife. I'm his uncle. My name is Raymondo, too. He was named for me."

Emily's felt her eyes grow wide, and backed away slowly while her heart thundered in her chest. Luke told her about his uncle and his involvement with the Mexican drug trade. "Leave me alone!" she shrieked. "Don't come near me."

A store security guard walked to them quickly. "Is there a problem, ma'am?"

"This man grabbed my arm!"

Icherra raised his hands. "It's a misunderstanding."

"Stay away from me. From us," she hissed at Luke's uncle. "We don't want anything to do with you."

"Do you know this man?" said the security guard.

"I've never seen him before, but I know of him. He's a criminal."

Icherra's eyes changed from warm brown to icy dark, and Emily shivered. "You should learn the meaning of respect," he snapped.

"Enough!" said the security guard. "That's enough out of you. Leave the store before I call the cops and have you arrested for assault."

Emily thought it was a wonderful idea to have Icherra arrested, but it looked like that wasn't happening. Icherra backed away, then turned and calmly walked out of the store.

"If you want to do your shopping," said the guard, "I'll keep an eye out and make sure he doesn't enter the store again. When you're done, tell the cashier to call me and I'll walk you out to your car."

She managed to grab the groceries she needed and appreciated that the guard carried them as he walked her to her car. Her heart racing, she thanked him for the millionth time and drove off, locking her doors and watching her review mirror the entire ride back.

She was still shaking when she arrived home. She took the bag with the stuff for dinner and left the rest for Luke to bring in when he got home. Nervously, she looked around the parking lot to check her surroundings. She wished fervently that Luke was home now, but the last thing she wanted to do was upset him while he was at work. He'd rush home and then worry obsessively about his uncle showing up.

And she didn't want to set her little sister off, who called just as she put the groceries on the table. Angela the snitch would call Luke and fill him in on everything, spinning things into a situation much worse than it was, upsetting her on-edge husband.

"Is everything okay?" Angela asked. "You sound off."

"No, I'm fine," Emily insisted. "I just need to put my feet up, is all. I got a little tired at the store and decided to take a nap. It's not like they need me at the shop."

"You know what the doctor said. If your blood pressure goes up any more, he'll put you on bed-rest."

"Yes," sighed Emily, "I'm aware."

"Don't dismiss this, Em. This is your life and the baby's we're talking about."

"Sometimes you sound just like Dad." The words flew out of her mouth in a bitter tone. Immediately Emily regretted it. She shouldn't snipe at Angela because her sister had a better relationship with him than she did. Then again, Sam Dougherty wasn't her biological father; just the man who'd married her mom when she was pregnant.

"Well, maybe I should. You don't seem to be taking your condition seriously."

"It's not a condition—yet. And I do take it seriously. I just don't want to talk about it 24/7, okay?" Even Emily heard the peevishness in her voice, but really, who was the older sister here? She was tired of how her family treated her, like she was going to screw up at any time.

"Okay, Em. I'm just worried, is all."

"Luke worries enough for the whole family. Believe me, if he thought I wasn't okay he'd close the shop and be right here with me." She sighed and blew her bangs off her forehead. "I'm sorry, Ange. I'm just tired and cranky. I don't mean to be complaining. I'm being horrible. Sorry."

"Complain away, sis. I don't mind and I'll let you get away with it for another eight weeks," Angela chuckled. "You'll be at Sunday dinner, right?"

Sunday dinner wasn't just a ritual at the Dougherty house; it was a rite as holy as a Catholic mass, at least in the eyes of their mother. "How can we not?"

"Awesome! See you then."

Dredging and browning the beef for the stew and peeling and cutting the potatoes gave her something to do to take her mind off this threat. But the back of her mind mulled over the problem, and in the end she decided that she needed to call Matt Stone and let him know about this latest development. He might not be able to do anything directly about Icherra, but he had a way of explaining things to Luke that made sense to her husband.

Just as Luke wanted, she made sure the stew was low in salt, going so far as to use a low-salt beef broth for the base. She found it hard to eat a low-salt diet. Foods just didn't have the flavor without the demon salt, but she recognized that it was important for her baby's health, so she followed her doctor's advice. Just one salty item was enough to pack on the water weight, which drove up her blood pressure.

She rubbed her stomach. "Just a couple more months, baby, and we can get back to normal." Whatever normal was. She had no idea anymore.

After combining the meat, potatoes, a couple quartered onions, and a bag of baby carrots in the crock pot, she turned the appliance on high and sighed with relief. The slow-cooker would take care of the rest. Now she could put her feet up.

Only now she was keyed up and everything she looked at needed cleaning. The bathroom got her started when she spied toothpaste dried in the sink. Then, naturally, the toilet needed cleaning. Then the bedroom needed straightening, the living room dusting, and the kitchen a good wiping down of all the surfaces. She damp-mopped the kitchen and the bathroom floors before she decided the apartment was clean enough. Nesting, her mother would call it.

By now the delicious smell of stew cooking wafted through the rooms, reminding Emily that she hadn't eaten anything for lunch. She started for the kitchen when the edges of her vision started to go dark, and she felt lightheaded.

"Oh boy," she said out loud. "I guess I pushed myself too hard." She groped for the edge of the sofa, trying to steady herself, but her knees gave way. Everything seemed fuzzy and far away as she slid slowly to the floor.

And then everything did go dark.

"BP one-ninety over a hundred, patient unresponsive on the scene, collared and boarded because of a suspected fall."

Emily blinked and tried to get her bearings. She couldn't move and this frightened her, especially since her body jolted in a swaying motion that made her stomach sick.

"Where am I?" she croaked. "Where's my husband?"

"Try to relax, ma'am. You're in an ambulance en route to Middletown hospital. Your husband is following us in his car. He found you passed out when he came home from work. Can you tell me what happened?"

"I don't know. I felt dizzy, and I don't know, like everything was far away. My legs gave out. I don't remember how long I was out."

"He said you have a history of pre-eclampsia?"

"Not really. My blood pressure has been a little high, but the doctor was watching it. Really, is this board necessary? It's very uncomfortable."

"We'll be at the hospital soon," the paramedic said. He took her blood pressure again. "What has your blood pressure been?"

The ambulance slowed down and stopped with a lurch.

"Around one-thirty-five over ninety."

The paramedic's face remained neutral as he looked at the Sphygmomanometer's display. "Okay, ma'am, we're pulling into the hospital now. We'll get you right in."

The paramedics rolled her out of the back of the ambulance, and the cold Connecticut winter air hit her. She shivered, and they quickly pushed her in to the entrance of the emergency room. The smell of antiseptic hit her and she heard the cries of pain from one patient, making her gut clench in dread. She tried to quell the thought *what if I'm really sick*, but it was nearly useless. She had pushed herself too hard and her traitorous body used the opportunity to fall apart.

In a flash Luke was at her side, his face flushed from running to her.

"Please, sir. This entrance is only for hospital personnel."

"She's my wife."

"And they'll let you in at the desk when you tell them that."

"I'll be right in, Emily."

Emily swallowed hard, the gravity of the situation hitting her. She had fainted, and it was probably her own fault. She should have rested. Emily was sure the unexpected appearance of Luke's uncle didn't do anything to help the situation. But even that scary event receded in the face of the threat that hung over her head now. This was real, and it was dangerous, as evidenced by her very high blood pressure. Her own body was not handling this pregnancy well. She was very lucky she hadn't had a stroke. Fear spread a cold chill through her.

The paramedics wheeled her into a cubicle and some nurses moved in behind them.

"Just relax; we're going to move you onto the bed."

"Can we get me off this board?"

"Not until the doctor checks you out," said a nurse in blue scrubs. She smiled reassuringly at Emily. "I'm Ellen, and I'll be your nurse tonight."

"You make it seem like I'm going to be here all night."

"Well, maybe not all night. Most likely the doctor will order a bunch of tests for you, and we'll have to monitor your blood pressure for a while. We'll just have to see how things go. But we *are* going to take good care of you."

While the nurse fixed a blood pressure cuff to Emily's arm, Luke entered the room. His expression was near frantic as he took in the sight of Emily lying on the hard board, with the nurse rapidly affixing different instruments to Emily.

"Emily," said Luke. "How're you feeling?"

"Very embarrassed right now. This is a lot of fuss over a little fainting."

A little smile turned up the corners of the nurse's mouth. "I wouldn't say that. But let's get some information for your chart, and then I'll have someone come in from registration to take your billing information."

"Oh," groaned Emily, thinking that Angela would be on her shift soon. The last thing she wanted was for Angela to know about this. "Can you make sure it's not Angela Dougherty?"

"You know Angela?"

"Yes, she's my sister."

"Oh, okay, sure. I'll see what I can do."

"Thanks."

When the nurse left, Luke took her hand. "I'm sorry."

"Sorry, baby? You have nothing to be sorry about."

"Last night..." He didn't finish the words, but the look on his face was pure anguish.

"Sssh, sweetheart. That had nothing to do with it. You can bend me over the couch anytime."

"I shouldn't have."

"Luke Wade," she said sternly, "if you ever say anything like that again, you'll break my heart. I'll always want to make love to you."

He swallowed but seemed to only half hear her words. Luke stroked her hand.

"Pull up that chair and sit. You're making me nervous standing there."

"Sure, sweetheart." He dragged the metal and plastic chair closer to her bed and twined his fingers with hers. With that, they both began the long vigil in the emergency room, waiting for the verdict on Emily's condition.

CHAPTER FIVE

The Scary Situation

"Emily!" Angela poked her head in the doorway of the cubby. "What're you doing here? What happened? Are you okay?"

Luke picked up his head toward his sister-in-law, and Emily groaned. She shifted in the bed. The doctor had come in earlier; a slightly harried man not much older than Emily who looked her over and ordered a bunch of tests and IV fluids. Hospital staff had long ago relieved her of the pernicious spinal board, though she remained hooked up on the blood pressure cuff, an oxygen sensor, and now some IV fluids that rolled through her body and spiked her need to use the bathroom.

"I'm fine. Just fainted, is all."

Angela clucked at the lie.

"And don't you tell Mom and Dad."

Angela shook her head. "Already did. They're on the way."

"Angela!"

"You really didn't expect me not to tell them, did you? You're in the emergency room, for heaven's sake."

Emily groaned again and Luke squeezed her hand. She was tired, hungry, and upset. The last thing she wanted or needed was her parents' prying. Sam Dougherty didn't accept Luke as his son-in-law and Amanda Dougherty just accepted her husband's attitude. No. Emily definitely did not need her parents here.

"Luke," said Emily. "Can you find a nurse?"

"Sure, baby." He gave her hand a kiss. When he left the hospital room, Emily turned her eyes towards her meddling sister.

"What the hell, Angela!"

"Don't get mad at me. If I didn't tell them I'd be in the doghouse!"

"When they come, tell them I can't have visitors."

"I won't do that, Emily. They're worried sick. They've been..." Angela stopped and put her hand over her mouth, as if she didn't intend those words to fly out of her mouth.

"What? Since the wedding?"

Angela stood straighter and looked directly into Emily's eyes. "Since you met up with Luke again. Look, I understand. You love him. He loves you. But that shootout you were in did nothing to redeem Luke in their eyes. He still belongs to that motorcycle club. Emily, when is Luke going to grow up?"

"Get out!" said Emily. "You won't speak about my husband like that." At that moment, the automated blood pressure cuff decided to puff in preparation to take readings. It cut into her arm painfully as the cuff tightened to reach the maximum level of Emily's pressure.

"Emily, look..."

"Out!" Behind Emily, the monitors keened a warning.

Luke walked back into the room and took in the strained tableau between Emily and Angela. "What's going on?"

"Nothing. Angela was just leaving."

Angela gave her a cold stare, and, with a toss of her long black hair, stalked out of the room.

"What was that about?"

Emily sighed. "My meddling family."

A nurse came in, gave her a visual inspection, and turned off the monitor. "You shouldn't move around."

"I'm not. But I do need to use the bathroom."

"I'll get a bedpan."

"But I can walk."

"Of course you can, honey. But your blood pressure is high. The doctor wants you in bed until we get the results of the tests."

"When will the doctor come back in?" said Luke. "We've waited a while."

"Soon," was all the nurse said. She pulled out a bedpan from the cabinets hanging on the wall. She looked at Luke.

"You can come back in after your wife is finished."

"I'll be back, baby. I'll get a cup of coffee."

"You might as well get something to eat too," said the nurse. "You might be here a while."

Emily groaned as the nurse put the bedpan under her.

While he was with Emily, Luke did his best to look calm and composed. His wife would only freak out more if she knew how scared he was.

When he'd seen Emily crumpled on the living room floor, his heart stopped in his chest. Only when he saw her breathing could he catch his own breath. Though he loved their child, he cursed the day he was careless enough not to put on a condom all those months ago. Had he known even for a second that Emily could get so sick bearing his child, he'd never allow it. He was supposed to protect her, and his carelessness now threatened her life and their child's life. Luke would never forgive himself, especially if something happened to either of them.

Loving Emily was easy. Realizing how wedded she was to his soul was not. Losing her would cleave him in half. He realized that when he saw her passed out on the floor. This was not how he envisioned his life, which was once carefree and independent.

Not that he'd wanted things any other way now. He did try during the summer to cast her from his life for her own good. He was into too much shit with the DEA, Rojos, and Hombres to make it safe for her to be with him. It was the most miserable summer of his life. He didn't eat, didn't sleep, and didn't enjoy riding his motorcycles. It was as if he'd died and just walked around in a meat suit. He came alive again when she showed up in the Spawn's clubhouse with the message that she carried his child.

He couldn't lose her again or lose his child.

This married thing was damned hard. This being a parent thing was even harder.

He found the cafeteria and shuffled through the food line, but nothing looked good to him. Out of habit he purchased a burger from the grill, and some fries. He moved toward the checkout when someone rudely bumped him, nearly causing him to drop his tray.

"Sorry, man," said a gravelly voice.

Luke turned, ready with a volley of sharp words, and stopped short. His mouth gaped opened. It had to be a freakin' ghost. Standing before him was Gibs; from the shabby clothes to the long, gray, straggly beard.

"Gibs?" he said.

"Do I know you, man?"

Luke saw subtle differences now. The man had a scar near his right eye that Gibs didn't have. One front tooth was chipped.

"Sorry. You look like someone I knew."

"I had a brother. People said we looked a lot alike. His name was Frank."

"Oh, then you're Robert."

The man grunted. "Rob. How did you know him?"

"He worked for me."

"Yeah, the motorcycle shop." The man stared at him hard. "So, you're Luke. Helen told me about you."

"Helen?" Guilt stabbed him then and he suddenly lost what little appetite he had. Luke hadn't seen Gibs' wife for several months, even though he had resolved to keep in touch.

"Yeah, I came back to settle up with Frank's estate. She's a bit upset about that; got heart palpitations, so I brought her in."

Luke moved to the cash register and paid for his food, with Rob following him. "I see," said Luke, gritting his teeth. He felt uneasy next to this man who seemed at ease discussing this subject with a relative stranger. If he was like this all the time, no wonder Helen got upset. Gibs' wife didn't deserve any upset, not since she lost her husband. And certainly not from a brother-in-law who hadn't spoken to either Helen or Gibs for many years.

"Let me ask you," said Rob, "you handling the sale of Frank's bike?"

"Yes. Helen asked me to."

"But it's not sold yet?"

"Not a great time of year to sell bikes. There're several bike nights in the spring. I was going to take it then."

"Well, you might not have to bother. I might take it to settle part of my share."

"Share?" said Luke. He couldn't believe this asshole was discussing Gibs' possessions like they were his.

"Yeah. I'm his only living relative."

We'll see about that, thought Luke. If he had to pay Matt Stone himself, he wasn't going to let this bozo take anything away from Helen.

"Besides his wife, of course."

"Yeah, besides Helen."

"So where is she?"

"Emergency room. They'll let her out soon I think. I'll take her home then."

Luke resolved he'd check on things to see what he could do. It couldn't do Helen any good to have this creep hanging around her. "Well, I've gotta go."

"Great meetin' ya," said Rob, with a grin that could have been copied from Gibs' face.

Luke's gut clenched, being unable to reconcile his feeling of dislike for this man with the image that parroted his dead best friend. "Same here," said Luke as he slammed his uneaten burger and fries in a nearby garbage can. He moved as quickly as he could away from the man who was the specter of the man who died for Luke.

The doctor came in while Luke was getting something to eat.

"Mrs. Wade, the IV magnesium seems to be doing the work. Between that and the diuretic, your blood pressure, except for a spike, is coming down. We will keep you for observation for a few more hours, but I see no reason for you not to go home tonight."

"That's great news."

"Provided you stay on bed-rest until you see your obstetrician, which will be tomorrow at noon. I've called your obstetrician and let him know your condition. Most likely with symptoms like these, you'll be on bed-rest for the rest of your pregnancy, have to keep to a strict low-salt diet, and take medication as prescribed."

"What do you mean by bed-rest? There are so many things to do for the baby. And Christmas is coming up."

"Sorry, Mrs. Wade. Whatever needs to be done, you'll have to get other people to do for you. Your most important job is keeping you and your baby healthy."

Emily sank back into the pillow with a feeling of defeat. Her body had betrayed her. It couldn't keep her or the baby healthy without the doctors hovering over her. There were things she wanted to do before the baby came. Now her life was on permanent hold.

"Thank you, doctor," she said. As he left, tears slid down her cheeks. This wasn't right. It wasn't fair. She'd gone through so much this year: her ex-boyfriend making her life hell, reuniting with and then losing Luke, the shootout where Gibs died, finding out she was pregnant, Luke getting shot and nearly dying—and now this? It was all too much.

"Hey," said Luke as he walked back into the room. "What's this?"

"The doctor said I had to stay on bed-rest until the baby comes."

"Really," said Luke. "That's not so bad."

"Not for you! I'm not allowed to go anywhere or do anything. And there's so much to do to get ready for the baby, and then Christmas too."

"You know, they have this new thing called the Internet. I hear people shop on it all the time. Ships right to your door." He grinned. "You'll be fine."

"Luke! It's not Christmas if I can't shop the malls."

"It'll be Christmas, baby. Our first Christmas together, and I want to make sure that happens. You'll do exactly as the doctor says. There's no discussion about it."

CHAPTER SIX

Life and Death

Emily had to use the bedpan again, and the nurse shooed Luke out of the room again. He went to hunt for Helen and found her a few rooms down. The blond-haired fifty-ish woman lay with her head up in the hospital bed, looking tired and upset.

"Hey," said Luke.

"Luke, oh my lord." She sounded distressed. "What're you doing here?"

"Emily fainted, but I heard you were here too and thought I'd check up on you."

"Oh, it's nothing... Just some arrhythmia. My heart galloped there for a few minutes, but I'm okay now. I was more frightened than anything else. Nothing like that ever happened to me before."

"I saw Gibs' brother in the cafeteria."

Helen hissed in a breath. "Yeah. That guy won't leave me alone."

Luke moved into the room, closer to her bed. "Helen, you should have called me."

"You have your own stuff to deal with, Luke. I can deal with Frank's brother."

"He talks like he owns half of your stuff, Helen." *If not all of it.*

"Yeah, well, according to the law he owns some of it."

"I have a very good lawyer, Helen. I'll have him call you."

"Okay, on one condition: You don't pay that man a cent. I'll take care of my own bills."

"Now, Helen."

"No! You have enough on your plate with winter business dropping off and a new baby coming, plus paying for your own wedding."

"Who told you that?"

"It's a small town, Luke. Don't think the ladies at the knitting club don't talk about how Sam Dougherty is footing the bill at the Westfield Country Club for Angela's big-time spring wedding, but you and Emily had yours at the Hades' Spawn clubhouse. And don't give me that 'Emily wanted to keep it small' crap. No bride wants to keep her wedding to the love of her life small."

Luke felt the color rise in his face. The last thing he wanted was he and Emily being the topic of small town gossip. "Helen, Emily and I were very happy with our wedding. And we have what matters—each other. So don't think we were deprived in any way. And Emily did want to keep it small." He grinned at her and Helen smiled back.

"Still, what I say goes," said Helen, wagging her finger at Luke. "Don't you dare give that lawyer any money. It's bad enough that I took that money from you after Frank's funeral."

"I told you it was a bonus."

"And I told you that story was bullshit."

"Yes, ma'am," said Luke, relenting. He wasn't going to cross a sick woman now. "How long do you think you'll be here?"

"I think they're letting me go soon. At least that's what the doctor says."

"I'll give you a ride home."

"You don't have to."

"No, I want to. There's no need to spend any more time in Rob's company than necessary."

Helen sighed. "You're right. The man does raise my blood pressure."

The damned monitor kept going off, and the nurse came in each time to turn it off, her face carrying that professional mixture of detached observation with a shadow of concern that healthcare personnel often wore. Right now, the nurse fussed over the lines in Emily's arms, pursing her lips like something was wrong. Emily didn't know what set her nerves on edge more: lying in this hospital bed with tubes in her arms, the prospect of her parents showing up, or the feeling of failure that pervaded her mood.

Other women had babies without a single problem. Why did her body decide it had to be so difficult in doing what it was designed to do? Why couldn't she have her baby in the normal way?

"Are you hungry, Emily?" said the nurse.

Emily groaned. She remembered the stew in the crock pot set on high. Whatever was in there would now be a lumpy mess. Her stomach growled loudly, answering the nurse's question. "A bit, I guess." She grinned, despite how awful the day had become. "Seems my stomach speaks for itself."

The nurse chuckled. "I'll see what the kitchen can send. At this time of night, it's usually just sandwiches."

"That fine," said Emily, resting her head back against the pillows, feeling tired and defeated. She wanted to go home and curl up in Luke's arms, go to sleep, and forget all about this crazy day.

From outside her room came the sounds of paramedics rushing in. She heard the sounds of static-filled police radios, and someone calling out stats. A gurney rushed by, and then another as nurses ran after them.

Oh great, thought Emily, who had heard a few ER tales from Angela. Real emergencies rolled in, which meant that she'd wait even longer to get out while the ER staff worked in life or death situations.

As if things couldn't get any worse, her parents walked into the room.

"Oh, Emily," said her mother, looking over Emily with worry in her face.

"Mom, Dad," Emily said, relenting while her mother kissed her cheek. "You really didn't have to come."

"Nonsense," said Sam Dougherty. "You're our daughter. And you're in trouble."

"I'm not in trouble. I had a little fainting spell."

"Yes," said her father. "That's why they have a bunch of tubes in your arm."

"They do that to everyone," said Emily exasperatedly. Her parents always drove her to the edge of reason. They'd treated her like she was damaged goods since the day she was born, unable to think or do anything for herself. For many years their treatment of her caused her to distrust her own feelings and actions. In high school, when they insisted she give up Luke, she rolled right over and played the good girl, once again, to her unending unhappiness.

Before the shootout at the Hades' Spawn clubhouse, she'd learned the reason. Her mother had made a mistake with the wrong young man and ended up with Emily. Sam Dougherty loved Amanda enough to marry her, regardless of whether she carried another man's child. But both parents were overprotective in raising her, trying to ensure that Emily didn't grow up to make the same mistakes her mother did.

It seemed that Emily was doomed to hit a wayward path anyway, especially when she met Luke Wade in high school. And since she reunited with, then married, Luke seven years later, there wasn't an encounter when Sam Dougherty didn't treat Luke like he was bent on ruining Emily's life.

She couldn't take it. Not today. Not after everything that had happened. "Please," she said, barely containing her tears. "Just go home. I'll call you tomorrow. I promise."

"Oh, honey," said her mother. "We're here for you."

Emily barely knew what to say. They weren't listening to her—again.

"Sam, Amanda," said Luke as he walked back into the room.

"Hello, Luke," said Amanda unenthusiastically.

"Has the doctor said anything?" asked Sam. Emily swallowed, feeling bitter that the man who called himself her father wouldn't ask her directly.

The blood pressure cuff tightened on Emily's arm again, and, after it deflated, the damned monitor went off again. Emily craned her neck to see the reading, and cringed when she saw it back up to one-hundred-ninety over one-hundred.

"You know," said Luke. "All this excitement isn't helping Emily. Why don't you guys head home and we'll call you when we know something?"

Sam and Amanda Dougherty just stared at Luke as if he'd suggested they should rob a bank.

The awkward tension between Luke and her parents and the repetitive keening of the hospital monitor brought Emily to the breaking point. But before she could react, the nurse swept into the room.

"You'll all have to get out of here," she said crisply, to the point of rudeness.

"I'm her husband," protested Luke.

"Well, you can stay then, but you and you," she pointed to Amanda and Sam, "you need to go."

"But we're her parents," said Amanda.

The nurse nodded. "I understand, but the emergency room is not set up for visitors. If you stay, you'll have to stay in the waiting room."

"Bye, honey," said Amanda.

Sam just waved. "Later," he said.

"Call us," said her mother.

"Yes, Mom," Emily said weakly.

Reluctantly, her parents left, and the harried doctor swept in once again. He looked at the blood pressure readings. "Okay nurse, give her the Demerol we discussed earlier. I have it in her chart. That will get her blood pressure down."

"Doctor?" said Luke.

"With her blood pressure spiking like this, I'm admitting her to the hospital overnight. We need to keep that baby safe. There's no way I'm comfortable sending her home. It's more a precaution than anything. I'm sure with a night of rest, she'll be fine." The doctor gave Luke a reassuring smile, but to Emily's eyes Luke was near panic.

"Sure," said Luke. "Whatever it takes."

"Her obstetrician will see her on rounds in the morning, which is better anyway. We'll reassess her then and go from there. Trust me, it's much better to treat pre-eclampsia aggressively than waiting to see what it does. I'll put in the order for admission now and the nurses will get you settled in your room shortly."

The doctor and the nurse swept out the room purposefully.

"I'm sorry," said Emily.

"What? Baby, no. You've nothing to be sorry about."

"But I want to go home and be with you. I don't want to stay in the hospital." Even to her own ears she sounded tired and peevish, but she couldn't help it. The day was much too much for her frazzled nerves.

"You let the doctors and nurses take care of you and our baby. That's the most important thing right now." Luke took her hand, curled her fingers in his, and gave her a kiss on the cheek. "If anything ever happened to either of you, I couldn't take it."

It took another hour before an orderly came to wheel Emily to the maternity floor. Before that time, the nurse put Demerol in her IV and soon Emily had a silly grin in her face. "Wow," she said, utterly relaxed. "I feel great."

Luke wished he had something like that too, since his nerves were on a ragged edge.

When the orderly arrived, Emily giggled. "Looks like I'm going to take a ride," she said.

"So you're going to have a baby, eh?" said the orderly brightly.

"No, not yet," said Luke. "It's too early."

"Oh. Sorry."

The orderly didn't say anything else until they got to the room. While the orderly lined up the gurney with the hospital bed, two efficient-looking nurses swept in. One of them looked Luke up and down.

"You the father?"

"I'm her husband, so, yeah," said Luke.

"Well, visiting hours are over. You'll have to come back in the morning."

Luke sighed and kissed Emily's cheek once more. "Have to go, baby."

Emily's lips formed a pout, something she never normally did, but she was under the influence of the Demerol. "I'll miss you, baby," she said, and giggled.

Luke left the room with a heavy heart, sick with worry. He looked over his shoulder as he left to see the nurses lift her to the bed. They wouldn't even consider letting her put her feet on the floor just to get into bed. A clock at the nurses' station said it was nearly midnight, and Luke decided to see if Helen was still in the hospital so he could make good on his promise to take her home.

"Oh, perfect timing," said Helen when he arrived. "I just have to get my clothes on and I can leave."

"Great, I'll go warm up the truck."

"Where's Emily?" asked Helen.

"They're keeping her here overnight. I'll wait outside, and when you come to the Emergency entrance I'll drive the truck up."

"Thanks, Luke. This means the world to me."

"It's nothing."

In the grand scheme of things, it was nothing, nothing compared to the sacrifice Gibs had made so that Luke could keep living. Every time he thought about it, his gut clenched.

Luke wended his way out to the waiting room and then to the entrance of the department. The door slid open with a hiss and the cold November night hit him in the face. He pulled up his collar on his Hades' Spawn jacket, so he didn't see who was leaning against the wall at the entrance, though he did smell cigarette smoke.

"Hey, *pendejo*, you not going to say hello to me?"

Only one man called Luke *pendejo,* which had different regional meanings in Spanish, mostly along the lines of "stupid," "idiot," or "jackass." But from this particular criminal, it meant "asshole."

Luke whirled to see Pez, the man who acted as the intermediary between the MC club and the Rojos and the Hombres. He was one of the few who had membership in both gangs. He was sent to Westfield in August to straighten out the problem caused by Luke's old president, Jack Kinney, and the Rojos and the Hombres. But Pez's solution, to let everyone shoot it out between themselves, nearly cost Luke his life. He didn't trust Pez a single iota.

"Didn't expect to see you here," said Luke coldly. This was turning out to be one hell of night.

"A couple of my boys got in a knife fight."

Luke nodded. "I meant here in Middletown. Don't you live in Bridgeport?"

"After the Westfield Rojos clubhouse was cleaned out, I decided to take up residence there." He flicked his spent cigarette to the ground and lit another one. He offered his pack to Luke, but Luke waved him off.

"No; gave them up a long time ago," said Luke.

Pez shrugged.

"So," said Luke, "Bridgeport not big enough for you?"

"Nah, moved up." He turned so Luke could see the back of his leather jacket that sported a leering red devil in the center, the word "Rojos" in a top-arched rocker, and the words "Central Connecticut" in the bottom rocker.

Luke's jaw set. Of course Pez would have a three-piece patch, the mark of a criminal MC club. It was bad enough when the twenty or so Westfield Rojos occupied that clubhouse, but Pez being president of a newly formed and larger charter was another leap in size of criminality in Luke's little town. Pez waved his hand toward Luke. "But I see you've come down in the world." He pointed to Luke's jacket, which sported a two-piece patch, the mark of a social motorcycle club. Kinney had instituted a three-piece patch in his short reign as the president of Hades' Spawn.

"I told you before, Pez. The Spawn want no trouble with the Rojos."

"I was told you won't be," said Pez casually. He took a long draw on his cigarette.

Luke's eyes narrowed. "Who told you that?"

"Your wise guy friend. What's his name? Saks vouched for you with his leadership."

Fuck, thought Luke. Saks was related by blood to the wise guy, but he told Luke he wasn't involved with them. Maybe Saks lied.

"But don't be fooled," said Pez. "Lil' Ricki still wants your ass."

Luke stared at Pez, well aware that the incarcerated Rojos state president had made threats against Luke's life for imagined wrongs. Luke, however, didn't worry too much about him. One, Lil' Ricki declared that only he was allowed to seek revenge against Luke. Two, Lil' Ricki still had twenty years on his sentence.

"Whether or not he gets it is another story," said Luke.

"We'll see about that, *cabron*. We'll see about that."

CHAPTER SEVEN

Closing Time at the Red Bull

"Luke," said Helen as she slid into the toasty warm SUV, "you're an absolute prince." She shivered. "It's so cold tonight; it goes right through the bones." She wrapped her arms around herself, drawing her beige camel coat close to her.

"And it's only November," replied Luke. He glanced out of his window to see Pez give him a quick wave. Luke flexed his fingers on the steering wheel while clenching his jaw, and turned out of the Emergency Room parking lot.

"How's Emily?" asked Helen.

"She's okay. They just want to keep her under observation overnight."

"Uh-huh," she replied, obviously not believing him. "Luke, we've known each other a long time. You don't have to put on a brave front for me."

Luke didn't want to talk about this. Telling people made his wife's situation all too real. He was aware of the implications of her condition and it shook him deeply to his core. Luke couldn't, wouldn't recognize that anything bad would happen to the woman he loved. But Helen was family, just like his wife and his club were. "She's got a condition: pre-eclampsia."

"Yes," said Helen slowly, "I know what it is. My niece had it with her first. How's her blood pressure?"

"That's why she was kept in. It kept spiking, both times when her sister and her parents rolled in. It upset her."

"She's lucky she has family that cares about her."

"And she'd be the first to agree," Luke chuckled, "but they're a little overprotective."

"Ah," said Helen, as if she understood. "So what does the doctor say?"

Luke sighed. "That she has to stay on bed-rest for the rest of the pregnancy. That is going to drive her nuts. She's always cleaning the apartment, even though it's just the two of us. Honestly, I don't see how two people can make as much dirt as she claims to clean."

Helen chuckled. "It's the female discerning eye. There isn't a speck of dust that escapes it."

"I guess. I don't see it."

"I'm sure you have other things to worry about."

Yes. He did have other things to worry about. Like the shop and its finances, his immigration problems, Anglotti and the wise guys watching him, and the rumored arrival of his crime-lord uncle. He didn't want to think about these things now. Luke tried to loosen his tense neck with a roll of his shoulders. "So how are you doing, really, Helen?"

"It's tough, you know. I still expect to hear his boots on the floors at six each night." And then more quietly, "I miss him."

"Yeah," said Luke, his throat thickening with his own emotions, "I do too."

"Some days I don't think I can make it through the day. It's overwhelming at times. I'll be doing something, and think "I have to tell Frank about that." Then I remember I can't tell him anything, and then a kind of blackness falls over me and I can't breathe."

Sadness gripped Luke as he thought about how Helen lost her husband because of him. It wasn't right. It wasn't fair. Neither Gibs nor Helen deserved their fate.

"And then," said Luke, "his asshole brother shows up. What's going on with that?"

"You tell me. One minute he's talking about settling the estate, and the other he can't be bothered with discussing terms."

"That's strange."

"What's even stranger is that he's taken a six-month lease on a sublet in town. He isn't planning on leaving any time soon and I can't figure out why."

"That *is* weird," agreed Luke. "So what's he asking for?"

"It changes from meeting to meeting."

"He talked about taking Gibs' bike."

"Oh, for heaven's freakin' sake," Helen said with exasperation. "If that's what he wanted, why didn't he say so?"

"He didn't ask you?"

"No."

"He might be Frank's brother, but I don't understand that man."

They drove the rest of the way in silence, both lost in their own worries. Luke glanced at the clock on the dashboard as Helen got out of the SUV, announcing it was nearly one o'clock in the morning. "Are you sure you're going to be okay?" asked Luke.

"The doctor told me to get some rest and to call him in the morning. I have the phone by my bed. If I have a problem, I'll call 911."

"Okay, Helen. Call if you need anything."

"And you too, Luke," called Helen as she stood poised to close the door. "If you or Emily need something, you call me. I mean it."

"Thanks, Helen. I'll let you know what happens with Emily."

She smiled. "You do that, mister, or you'll be hearing from me."

Helen closed the door with a smile and a solid thud. To make sure she was safe, Luke watched as she walked into the house. When her inside light went on, he pulled out of the driveway. At the corner, he was about to drive right to take him back to his apartment. He didn't want to do that, to go back there and be alone without Emily next to him.

Instead he turned left, in the direction of the Red Bull. He'd barely visited since that night when he and Pez left there on the way to rescue Saks from the Rojos. Knowing that the Red Bull was run by active wise-guy members didn't make him feel safe or comfortable. But tonight, when all manner of bad things happened today, he just wanted to sit in a familiar place, drink a beer, and then go home.

Entering the Red Bull felt like coming home. Though it was very late, there were still a few regulars scattered through the large bar. Nothing had changed in those few months. The large bar in the center of room still featured a stacked pyramid of different bottles of liquor, the taps for the beer were still shined to reflect the lighting hanging from the ceiling, and different colored and sized bras hung from the rafters.

Luke hung his Hades' Spawn jacket on the pegs by the door, since Rocco, the owner, had a rule about bikers removing their colors when they entered. Some of the other patrons greeted Luke as he made his way to the bar. He smiled at John, Rocco's brother and main bartender, and John broke into a bright grin.

"Luke! Where've you been hiding, man?" John knew very well that Luke had built his own small bar as part of the Hades' Spawn clubhouse. But since that was competition, both men avoided that part of the conversation. John drew Luke's favorite draft and slid it to him.

"Thanks," said Luke. "Do I still have a tab here?"

"Of course," scoffed John. "You have credit on it."

"Good to know." Luke pulled at his draft and eyed the bar. Here in the center of the room it was bright, but along the walls and in the corners the lighting was low. He couldn't quite make out who sat at different booths. "Any Rojos around?"

"Nope. We banned them."

"Really? You banned a whole MC club?" This was unprecedented. Rocco and John had been known to ban an individual or two, but rarely. A whole club, though? Wow.

"The familia didn't like them around. Troublemakers."

"So, they aren't doing business with them?"

"I didn't say that," said John. "Business is business, but I can't say more."

"And I don't want to know."

"Hey, Luke!"

Beer in hand, Luke turned to see Pepper, or rather DEA Agent Hector Garcia, walking toward him with a smile and his hand outstretched. Luke took it, though his smile was strained. Pepper had his Hades' Spawn jacket slung over his arm. There was nothing that Luke could do about Pepper's membership in the club. Luke was sworn to secrecy about his involvement with the DEA, and Pepper's membership was a consequence of the undercover work he did there. While Luke was in the hospital recovering from his gun- shot wound from the shootout at the Spawn's clubhouse, the other members of the club patched in Pepper. They had thought him a hero in his part in subduing Kinney, Dagger, and Wolf. But the other members of the club didn't know that Pepper was planted there to spy on them. Had they known, things might have turned out differently.

Luke had no desire to speak with Pepper now. The events of the day had left him raw enough that he wasn't fit company for most people. Pepper was a reminder that the DEA didn't follow through on their promises, and had left Luke hanging in immigration hell. In the aftermath of the cluster-fuck that was the shootout at the clubhouse, the DEA pinned the failed operation on Pepper. He was consigned to a desk assignment since then and showed up less frequently on Sundays to work with Luke in the shop. Luke had no idea what he was doing here now.

"Can we talk?" asked Pepper.

"Closing time soon," said Luke,

"Please."

Luke sighed. His nerves were frayed and his body pumped with too much adrenaline to have this conversation. But after the visit with immigration, he wanted some answers. Maybe Pepper had them. He pointed to a booth and settled into it. Pepper slid in after him. "Did you hear about the little home visit by immigration?" His face was hard with anger. If the DEA had lived up to their promises, he wouldn't be in this mess.

Pepper looked surprised. "No; sorry."

"Really? You guys knew enough about my life when you needed me." As sarcastic as that came out, he was even more bitter. His anger curled into a hard knot in his stomach.

Pepper looked away and Luke saw that the agent had no answers for him.

"What the hell, Pepper! The DEA promised to clear up my immigration status."

"Sorry; I can't help you. Moyes is in charge of that and we don't even work together anymore."

"Then why did you want to speak to me? Because right now there is precious little I want to hear from or say to you."

Pepper pursued his lips. "We hear that Oklahoma Walker is getting out soon."

"Really," said Luke after taking a sip of his beer. "I wouldn't know."

"He hasn't contacted you?"

"Okie made a rule when he went in. No contact."

"Why did he do that?"

"Probably because he knows how law enforcement likes to assume his friends are criminals too."

Pepper looked away, then back at Luke. "Okay, we deserve that. But we have it on good word that he's been talking to 'Lil Ricki in jail."

"So? I'm sure there isn't much else to do in the slammer." Luke was growing more annoyed with Pepper and this conversation. By the time he was done in here, there wouldn't be enough beer to settle him down tonight.

"Word is Walker made a deal with 'Lil Ricki to hang back while he extracts some revenge on the Hombres."

"Revenge?"

"Yeah, for Frank Gibson's death."

Luke was shocked. Yes, Gibs did get in the middle of the Hombres and the Rojos because of Jack Kinney. And the Hombres did send the men who ended up firing the fatal shot that Gibs caught. But it was craziness to take on a street gang the size of the Hombres. That meant certain death for every Spawn involved, and maybe the ones who weren't. "I don't believe it. Okie wouldn't do anything that crazy."

"Long-time friend? Bike brother? What do you think, Luke? Even social clubs go ballistic when one of their own is killed."

"What? You specialize in biker gangs?"

Pepper gave him a look of appeal that begged for Luke's understanding. "This is part of a broader investigation. And as far as this conversation goes, we never had it."

"What aren't you telling me, Hector?" said Luke.

"There's nothing I can tell you, but for your own and Emily's sake, be careful." He pushed up from the table and walked out of the bar, as casually as if was strolling on a summer beach.

Luke had a real what-the-fuck moment watching Hector leave. For the second time in six months, the skinny Hispanic surprised him. The first time was when he found out Hector was a DEA agent. That was a kick to the head. It took restraint on Luke's part not to kick his ass each day in the shop while they were playing their parts to reel in Jack Kinney. But this? What did "this is part of a broader investigation" mean?

On the day of the shootout Hector had told him he wanted to get out of the DEA, and asked if Luke would train him in motorcycle repair. But what happened was that Hector got blamed for the cluster-fuck of the shootout and was placed on desk duty. The DEA still signed his paychecks, though it was obvious they didn't want him there. If that wasn't a good sign to leave the agency, that, in effect, offered him an invitation to leave, why didn't he?

Unless... someone else had asked him to stay for another reason.

That wasn't good at all.

CHAPTER EIGHT

An Unwelcome Visitor

Luke thrashed the sheets off violently, waking with a start and breathing hard. A thin sheen of sweat covered him even though it wasn't hot in the room. The all-too-real nightmare gripped him in its frightening aftermath, and he lay there, reliving every detail.

He was eight, and playing in the schoolyard with the other children. Being more adventurous than the other boys, he hung upside down from his knees on the monkey bars, egging the other boys on to join him.

"Bet you can't do this," he said as he swung from his knees on the bar. They had laughed, but it was friendly, because Luke was the leader of the group. He had always pushed them to do things they wanted to do but were afraid to. In his little eight-year-old heart, he was proud and happy that these boys hung on everything he did.

"Come down, Ray," said his teacher, Miss Ryan.

Ray smiled. He liked Miss Ryan; okay, more than liked her. With her blond hair, pretty blue eyes, and warm smile, he thought she was the most beautiful lady he'd ever seen, aside from his mom, of course. But his mom was his mom. Miss Ryan was the sunshine in his day. His heart thumped whenever she paid attention to him, and so he made sure she paid attention to him. Someday he was going to marry Miss Ryan. He was sure of it.

But there was something in Miss Ryan's face today. Instead of her usual smile, her face was drawn and tense.

"Okay, Miss Ryan," he said. He gripped the monkey bars with his hands and swung off them with an easy drop to the ground.

She reached her hand out to him. "Come with me," she said in a tight voice.

Ray was confused. Had he done something wrong? He didn't remember doing anything wrong, but he took her hand. Any other day he would be ecstatic that his favorite teacher wanted to hold his hand. Now, a feeling of dread overtook him.

The other boys, unused to Miss Ryan's somber expression, hung back and didn't say a word. Ray looked over his shoulder as he left the play yard, and one of the boys awkwardly waved goodbye.

"Where are we going, Miss Ryan?" he said as they entered the school and started down the long corridor that cut from one end of the school to the front doors.

She didn't say anything.

"I'm sorry if I did anything wrong."

Miss Ryan stopped in the long hallway and bent to him, giving him a hug. Ray noticed she was crying, and he grew frightened. Why was Miss Ryan crying?

She swept his hair off his forehead with her hand, a gentle touch that showed she cared about him too. "You didn't do anything wrong, Ray. Nothing at all. You're a special boy, you know that? Remember that, okay?"

"Sure," he said, although his confusion increased, forming a knot in his stomach.

"Come on," said Miss Ryan. "They're waiting."

Ray didn't know who "they" were, but he didn't want to go where "they" were. Still, it was Miss Ryan taking him toward the principal's office. Miss Ryan wouldn't do anything to hurt him. Ray loved Miss Ryan and would do anything she asked.

Miss Ryan opened the door slightly and words tumbled out of the room.

"This can't be right," said Mrs. Cooper, the school principal. Her voice was terse. "I think we should call the school lawyers."

"This is a federal subpoena, ma'am," said a low, gruff voice. "You can call all the lawyers in the world, but they aren't going to help you against a federal judge's order."

The door opened wider and Mrs. Cooper stood behind her desk, looking very unhappy. A tall dark-haired man stood next to it. The man was so tall Ray had to crane his neck to see his face, only he couldn't see it because the brim of the man's hat threw shadows on his face.

"Ray," said Mrs. Cooper. "You'll go with Agent Harkness."

"Where's Mama?" said Luke, hiding behind Miss Ryan. "Where's Papa?" He didn't like the look of this man and wanted to go home.

"Ssh," said Miss Ryan. She picked up his backpack which sat on a chair in the corner. "I have all your things from the school room right here."

"Don't make me leave, Miss Ryan. I want to stay here with you. Mama'll come to get me after school. She always does."

"I'm sorry, Ray," she said with sadness in her voice. "There's nothing I can do. But I put my address in the backpack, so you write me, okay?"

"That won't be necessary," said the man gruffly. He stepped forward and took the backpack, and grabbed for Ray's hand. "He won't be allowed contact with anyone from his past."

"Agent," warned Mrs. Cooper, "you're scaring the boy."

"Good," growled Harkness, "because he should be afraid."

"Agent!" protested Mrs. Cooper.

Ray shrieked and ran out of the principal's office. He didn't want to go with this man. He'd find a place to hide. There was a place in the basement, behind the big old boiler, where he could scoot into but an adult could not. He'd stay there until the man went away. Mama and Papa would come. They wouldn't let this man take him away.

His feet slapped down the hallway, but the man was faster.

"Fuckin' A!" the man exclaimed as he reached around Ray's waist and lifted him off his feet. "Settle the fuck down, kid," he spit as Ray struggled. "There ain't nothing you can do, kid. You're coming with me."

"Mama! Papa!" Ray screamed as the man carried him out of the school and to his car. He practically threw Ray into the back of it, along with his backpack.

"Shut up, kid," said the man as he strapped Ray in with the seatbelt, roughly. "You ain't seeing your old man or mama ever again, so you might as well close your pie-hole."

The man climbed behind the wheel and his car rumbled to life.

"Why!" screamed Ray. "Why can't I see Mama and Papa?"

The agent turned in his seat and glared at Ray.

"Because they're dead, kid. Now shut the fuck up."

Luke scrubbed his face with his hands and then reached over to pull Emily to him. Only Emily wasn't there, and he panicked a minute before he remembered that his wife was in the hospital overnight.

Shit. Just that thought caused his gut to clench.

The smell of the burnt dinner permeated the apartment. He checked to find that it was off, and he breathed a sigh of relief that the words "with automatic shut-off" were printed under the brand name on the crockpot. He left it, too tired to clean it, and hit the bed.

For all the good it did him.

He turned on the light by the bed and sat up, and then realized the room was very cold. He shivered. It shouldn't be this frosty here. Luke pulled on the jeans that he'd left in a heap on the floor and went looking for the cause of the lack of heat. He found it. His front door was wide open.

"What the fuck?" he thought. He looked over the door jamb but didn't see any signs of forced entry. Maybe he forgot to shut the door completely when he came in? He certainly was exhausted when he arrived home from the hospital.

The click of a light switch caught his attention and he whirled to the sound. The light in the kitchen was blazing. Luke tensed. He definitely did not leave on the light there.

Luke looked around and found no one. He remembered the .45 in the gun safe in the closet to his right, but it would take longer to get it out than he had time for. It was ironic that the gun was sealed away for safety's sake when Luke had such a desperate need for it now.

With no weapons in hand, he decided to go for bravado.

"Who's there?" he called out as his heart hammered.

"You need better security," said a deep, gravelly voice with a Hispanic accent. The refrigerator door closed with a rattle of beer bottles on the door.

Luke shut the front door, though he wanted to flee. He had no idea who was in his apartment. Some Rojos or Hombre? Why would one venture into his apartment? Fury built in his heart. This was his home. How dare they break in! "Show yourself," Luke demanded with a growl.

"I would think," said the stranger as he came out of the kitchen with two beers in hand, "that you would greet your family better."

The intruder was elderly, maybe in his sixties, thin with salt and pepper hair. He cocked his head toward Luke. His skin was brown. "You look like her," he said. "That pale skin and those blue eyes."

"Who?"

"Your mother. She was a pretty thing, but not tough. Not like us Icherras."

"Raymondo," Luke hissed. "What the hell are you doing here?"

"Like your wife," the crime boss said with a sneer, "no respect."

"What do you mean by that? If you come near my wife, I'll—"

"You'll what, Raymondo? What will you do to me?" His dark eyes glittered with malice, and Luke nearly shivered looking into them. This was a man who was so cold that his very presence screamed danger.

"My name is Luke."

"Sure, *sobrino*; that's what it says on your driver's license, isn't it?"

Luke clenched and unclenched his hands at this side. How did this man know about his unfortunate name change on his documents? "What do you want?"

Icherra sat on the side chair and opened his beer.

"Just to connect with family, eh? It's been a long time since I've seen you, twenty-two; no, twenty-three years. You used to love your Uncle Raymondo. You liked to swim in my pool and eat empanadas for lunch."

"I don't remember a single thing about that," Luke grit out.

"No? Shame. In any case, you've done well for yourself. Your own business, eh? Connections with the Mafia and the Spic gangs."

"What the hell are you talking about?"

"You're married now, with a baby on the way. I would think you'd want to give your family everything you could. I'm a rich man in Mexico, *sobrino*. I can give you and your family many advantages. Me? Your cousin, my son, died last year. It's been a tough year and I'm getting old. I need family I can count on. Raymondo, it's time for you to come home."

A sick feeling hit Luke. This ass didn't expect he'd go to Mexico, did he? To run his business? What the fuck?

"Home?" said Luke slowly. "This is my home."

Icherra cocked an eyebrow at Luke. "I think the U.S. government thinks otherwise. My lawyers tell me you can't secure citizenship here. Too many impediments."

Luke's jaw set. The old man was blowing smoke up Luke's ass to get him to budge. But Luke wouldn't. Immigration would have to drag him kicking and screaming to Mexico. And he sure wasn't going to let his drug-running uncle lead him there. "I'm not going to Mexico, and the last thing I want is to get mixed up in your crooked business."

"No? If you did, I'd even let you keep that money my brother stole from me. It must've grown in the bank, eh?"

"Get out of my house."

Icherra sighed and put his beer bottle on the coffee table. "I can see you'll need some more convincing." He stood. "Well, it was good to see you, *mi reyito*."

"What? What was that you called me?"

"*Mi reyito*? Did you forget your native tongue? I used to call you that. Means, uh, my little king. But I think of it as "Little Ray." A play on your name, see?"

"I don't know you. And I don't want to know you. Don't you dare come near me or my wife."

"I cannot make that promise, Ray."

"My name is Luke."

"Yeah, sure. As the Americans say, see you around." Icherra strolled to the door and yanked it open to the chilly November pre-dawn. He left it open as he walked through it, and Luke took quick steps to it and slammed it shut so hard the door frame shook.

Anger blazed through him. What was he going to do, call the police? He was on the Westfield police department's official shit list, so that wouldn't help. To complain about what? That his uncle had visited him?

His drug lord uncle wanted him to work the business with him. Luke sank to the couch and kicked the coffee table hard. It teetered on its four legs then settled, but the beer Icherra was drinking fell and spilled onto the carpet. Swearing, Luke leaped up and got some towels from the bathroom, mopping up the mess.

The beer soaked into the carpet and Luke knew he'd have a hell of time cleaning the carpet. How could he get the smell out? Emily always seemed to know how to clean every little thing, but Luke was useless at it.

Just like he felt useless trying to straighten out his own life.

What the hell was he going to do now?

CHAPTER NINE

Evan

The baby kicked her hard in the stomach, waking Emily with a start. Junior must have been at it good all night because the inside of her belly felt sore. Must've had a soccer match going on inside her.

"Hey, kid," she said to her stomach as she opened her eyes groggily. She found to her dismay that her head pounded. "Can't you let your mama sleep?" She tried to straighten herself on the hospital bed, thinking that she might have slept on her neck wrong on the inclined head, but it only brought another round of nauseating headache pain. There didn't seem to be a way to escape it.

"How you doing, honey?" said a woman in nursing scrubs, walking in with the efficient stride of someone who had no time to spare. "I'm Evelyn, your nurse today." She appeared older than Emily, maybe in her late thirties or early forties. She stood around five-foot-two, and carried some extra weight around her middle. Her demeanor communicated that she took no nonsense.

"Hi," said Emily. "I'm okay. Just seem to have a bit of a nagging headache."

The nurse studied the monitors over Emily's head. "Let's take your blood pressure again."

"Again?" It felt like the thing was squeezing every twenty minutes through the night. She bit her tongue to keep from complaining. She didn't feel the least bit guilty acting peevish. The last twenty-four hours had been hellish, and she was sick of everything. She desperately wanted to go home, but keeping the odd comment to herself might get her out just that much faster.

Evelyn took off the cuff and adjusted it on Emily's arm. "It checks you every hour and records it. But it's what we do to keep you and your baby safe."

"I understand," said Emily with a resigned sigh.

"Now you just lay quiet there and don't move, so we can get a good reading."

It was then that Emily noticed something tugging at her from between her legs. Her free hand went down to check. "What the heck?"

"A catheter. With all that Demerol in you, you couldn't possibly walk to the bathroom. And with the fluid we gave you, you couldn't help but go."

"Oh geez," said Emily, feeling worse than ever. The cuff puffed and pressed painfully into Emily's arm. She took in a sharp breath.

"Relax into it," said the nurse. "This is good practice for Lamaze."

"I haven't taken any of the classes."

"Have you signed up?"

"No." She and Luke had barely gotten a break between the wedding and running the shop to think about birthing classes. Even though her doctor recommended them, she just didn't find the time to make that phone call.

"Well, we have one here in the hospital on Wednesdays. I'll get you information about it. The instructor works on this floor. I'll have her stop by."

"I wasn't planning on natural childbirth."

The nurse put a hand on her arm. "Glad to know there's one woman who admits it. But there are usually hours of labor in before they put in the block, and it's better knowing how to handle that part before you get to the endgame."

"Oh," said Emily. At that moment, she missed her mother. Luke was great, but there were some things only a mother would know or understand. She shouldn't have been so rude to her mom last night. Maybe it wasn't her mother who bothered her, but her father being there. She couldn't stand seeing the angry look in his eyes, staring at tubes and wires stuck in her. Emily felt like the defective daughter he'd always treated her as.

"Okay," said the nurse. "It's still a little high. We'll see what the doctor has on order for you to help with that. Are you hungry?"

Emily's stomach growled, answering that question. She laughed nervously. "I guess so."

"Okay, here's the menu." Evelyn pulled out a menu from the nightstand next to the bed and set the phone next to Emily. "Order what you like, though the diet staff will tell you if you can't have something. Hint: I think bacon is off the menu for you." The nurse said the last words lightly, trying to make a joke of it, but Emily didn't feel lighthearted.

"Do you think I can get something for this headache?"

"Sure, honey. Again, I have to check the chart and clear it with the doctor, but I'll get you something."

"That's great," said Emily, though she delivered the words unenthusiastically. She hated this cold, sterile room with no one but strangers around her. Desperately, Emily wanted to go home. She wanted her husband. "When are visiting hours, if you don't mind me asking?"

"Nine to nine."

"Oh." Would Luke come in then, or would he go to the shop? What would he do? Maybe she'd call him and find out, but no, it was only seven in the morning. She should let him sleep. He was up late too.

The nurse left, her soft-soled shoes squishing on the linoleum. Feeling miserable, Emily picked up the phone to dial the number for the kitchen and embarked on the adventure of finding what she could eat.

Half an hour later, Emily had her pillow over her eyes, trying to beat back her horrendous headache. The nurse hadn't returned yet, and it was the only thing she could think of to get some relief. She heard footsteps and then something hit the rolling utility table by her bed.

"Here's your breakfast," a masculine voice said softly. Through her headache, she thought something was familiar about that voice but she couldn't place it. She moved the pillow and stared at the tray. She lifted the cover, not looking forward to the food. Most of the breakfast items had too much salt for her diet. She ended up taking scrambled eggs, toast, and a bowl of oatmeal. The eggs and toast were cold and soggy. The oatmeal, which Emily didn't like much anyway, looked entirely tasteless.

She groaned unhappily.

"I hear," said the masculine voice from the doorway, "they make the food bad to encourage you to go home earlier."

Emily jerked her head up in shock. She could not see him because he hid in the alcove that led into the room that housed the bathroom. But she knew that voice very well.

"What the hell are you doing here, Evan?"

Evan Waters, with a smarmy smirk on his face, walked closer so Emily could see him. Her old boyfriend had not changed much since the spring, when she had kicked him to the curb. He had the same messy haircut, and he was still thin. She thought he was bad before then, when he laid his hands on her. But what he did after was worse. Evan had accused her of car theft, and stalked her relentlessly until he was arrested, threatening her. Indirectly he was the cause of her losing her job as well. However, though he attended the wedding ceremony, he had stopped his bad behavior. Until now.

He pointed to the white scrubs he wore. "I'm doing my community service here in the hospital. You know, the community service I had to do because of that threatening charge you put on me. I saw your name up on the board outside and thought I'd check up on you, Emily. Despite what you think and despite everything that happened to me, I do care about you."

"What happened to you?" Her voice was filled with disbelief. She couldn't believe he was twisting all that happened to make it sound like he was the injured party.

"Yes. Getting arrested. Getting beat up at that clubhouse of your husband's. As a matter of fact, I talked with my attorney yesterday about a wrongful injury suit. I *was* beaten up on your husband's property and my leg was broken. I had months of healing, and then physical therapy. It was all very expensive."

Emily's breathing tightened. He couldn't, he wouldn't do this, would he? Yes, Evan was enough of an asshole to do just that.

"And then," he continued, "there is pain and suffering. Someone has to pay."

"I'll show you some pain and suffering," spit Emily.

"I'll let that go," said Evan solicitously. "You've had a rough night, and it can't be easy living with a criminal. Or carrying his child."

"Luke is no criminal, and we love our baby." Her head started to pound more as she frantically searched for the nurses' call button in the blankets in the bed.

"Emily," he said, as if speaking to a small child, "if it walks like a duck and quacks like a duck, it's a duck."

"You're the one who saw the inside of the jail!" Her voice rose an octave as the need to get this man away from her blossomed into panic.

"Well, I didn't have the luxury of having friends in the DEA to clear *my* charges."

"What're you talking about?" Emily was in full-blown panic, breathing harder than she should. The alarms on the monitors went off, sending their screeches through the room.

"He didn't tell you? In exchange for being their snitch on the criminal activities in the Hades' Spawn, the DEA arranged for those charges, the charges you should have answered for, dropped."

"Luke didn't do that."

"Do the math, Emily. I did. But once your husband is bankrupt, and from what I understand, deported, things can get back to normal. I'll understand if you want some time after that, but eventually we'll be back together, just as we should have been."

"You're nuts. I'll never leave Luke. You and I will never be together."

"Oh, think again, Emily. Who else would want a single mother with a baby? But we loved each other once. We can do it again.

"Get out, get out!" screamed Emily. Her hands were shaking, and, while she found the call button, her hands couldn't seem to press the button properly.

Evan held up his hands. "Okay for now, Emily. I've got to get going anyway. Now, after working all night here, I've got to go to my job. But that's what happens when you get convicted of a crime. Get some rest, Emily. You're going to need it."

It felt like forever before Evan finally walked out, and then another eternity before the nurse came back.

Evelyn walked into the room faster than her previous pace, looking efficient and ready to tackle any problem. Emily was breathing hard, and the heart monitor was screaming. The damned blood pressure cuff went on again, cutting painfully into her arm. "What's going on, Emily?"

Emily couldn't speak as her breath caught and tears streamed down her face.

"Cup your hands over your nose and breathe deeply," instructed Evelyn calmly.

Following Evelyn's instructions, she sucked in her own breath, and slowly her breathing calmed. What didn't calm was her heart that raced with all the awful things that Evan said. She couldn't believe he came to her room, making threats and telling her that they'd be together again. The man was delusional.

Evelyn pulled oxygen tubes with nose plugs from the wall behind the bed and settled them over Emily's head.

"Here, a little oxygen will help you. Your oxygen level dropped with breathing that hard. Do you often have panic attacks?"

"Sometimes. Not in a while though." She hadn't had one since she and Luke had married.

"Well, you've been through a tough time here." Evelyn glanced at the monitors. "The doctor just started his rounds on the floor. You'll see him in a short while."

"I want to go home," said Emily. "I, I..." Her voice trailed off. She felt massively unsafe here now that she knew Evan worked here.

Evelyn patted her arm in a motherly fashion, which made Emily want her mother even more. The nurse's phone rang in her pocket, and Evelyn looked at the message on the screen.

"I have to go, but I'll be right back." Evelyn rushed out the door, leaving Emily alone with her cold breakfast and fearful thoughts. Her stomach churned, so she couldn't even contemplate eating that food. She didn't want to be alone here, and didn't know when Luke would show up. She picked up the handset of the phone, and dialed her parents' number. Thankfully it was her mother who answered. "Mom," said Emily.

"Emily, are you okay? The baby okay?"

"I'm fine, the baby's fine, but, Mom, can you come stay here with me a while?" She sniffled and wiped her tears from her eyes. "I don't want to be alone here."

CHAPTER TEN

Medicinal Donuts

Luke took a quick shower and dressed before checking his phone. He didn't see a message from Emily. He hoped that meant she was still sleeping and getting some much-needed rest. Then he noticed with a groan that Emily's phone was on the dresser. Maybe that's why she hadn't called. In the age of the smart phone, people didn't bother to remember phone numbers and she might not remember his. He put her phone in his jacket pocket in case she needed it, even though he wanted to bring her home today.

He admitted that he missed her terribly. The bed was cold and lonely without her. He was sure he wouldn't have had that nightmare if she was with him. He hadn't had any since she'd moved into his apartment.

Checking his phone, he realized it was Mrs. Diggerty's trash day. Emily had a soft spot for her former landlady, and for that reason Luke did what he could for the elderly woman. Mrs. Diggerty's was close enough on the drive to work that it usually wasn't a big deal to stop by to bring the trash to the curb on the way to work. But today Luke wasn't going to work.

And that thought made him remember that he needed to call Saks.

"What?" said Saks gruffly.

"Rise and shine. You're elected to open the shop today."

"Who is it?" said a feminine voice in the background.

"That bastard, Luke."

"Oh."

"Hey, asshole. That's your boss you're talking about."

"Yeah, a boss who won't give me a layoff so I can go to Florida. Bastard."

"Yeah, yeah. I do feel sorry for you."

"So what's up?"

"I had to take Emily to the hospital. They kept her overnight."

"Oh, sorry, man." Saks sniffed as if trying to clear his sinuses. "Yeah, I'll go open the shop. Is she okay?"

"I think so. They are just keeping her for observations."

"What happened?"

"What is this, twenty questions? I'll tell you later."

"Sure. Sorry, man. What time is it?"

"Seven, so you've got two hours to get there. Do you think you can make it?" Luke's voice came out sarcastic even to his ears, but he wasn't in the mood to be light-hearted. His wife was in the hospital, damn it, and he just wanted to get to her as quickly as he could. Sure, he wasn't supposed to be there before nine, but maybe he could sneak in. What would they say? Tell the husband and father he couldn't be there? Screw that.

"Hell, Luke," said Saks, sounding slightly annoyed. "You could have let me sleep."

"I've known you long enough to know that you and mornings don't agree."

"It's this damned seasonal affective disorder. I really need to get some sunshine."

"What you need is to be less of a smart-ass."

"Someone has not had his morning caffeine fix.

"Damn straight. Bye." Luke put his phone in his back pocket, locking the front door behind him. He turned up his collar as the raw morning air hit his unprotected face and hands. The sun was an icy blur in the gray sky and Luke shivered. *It feels like snow,* he thought as the chill worked into his blue jeans before he reached the SUV. While he let the truck warm up, he turned on his headset and waited for it to connect to his phone. Luke didn't want to miss a call from Emily, if, by some grace, she remembered his phone number. It took until he pulled onto the street before the Bluetooth kicked in.

And when it did, what he got was an earful.

"Ahh," he heard Saks say. "Um, I really have to get going."

"Oh, I'll get you going," the woman said in a seductive voice.

"Oh, fuck," thought Luke.

Saks started groaning. "You do that so good."

The woman made muffled sounds as if her mouth was full.

Hell, Saks was getting a blow job. Luke was at once amused and jealous. Just hearing Saks' enthusiastic responses teased his cock into stiffening.

Damn, I'm really missing my wife, he thought as he shifted uncomfortably in his seat.

Luke couldn't pull the phone from his pocket while he was driving, though he admitted that was a lame excuse anyway. One part of him wanted to listen, and another part of him wanted his woman working his dick like that. No part of him wanted to stop this, because it would make really good material with which to prank Saks.

"Ah, yeah, like that."

The woman's mouth was making loud slurps and smacks.

"You're so good, so good, baby.

Luke imagined Emily's pretty little lips around his cock, taking him in, her eyebrows scrunched as she concentrated on his pleasure. She did that sometimes, and he loved it each time. At times like that, when she gave so freely of herself, not thinking of herself, he felt to his core how much she loved him. She would grip the part of his cock with one of her dainty soft hands, and play with his balls as her mouth worked as much of him as she could take. His cock felt so good in her warm, wet mouth, especially when her tongue would rub against it, teasing out the intense sensations that only a good blow job could give. This would always send sparks up his spines. She made noises too, like she enjoyed the feel of him in her mouth. Thinking that would bring him close to the edge.

"Fuck," he heard through the headset. "I'm going to cum."

Luke was a little gone himself. He was driving on automatic, not noticing exactly where he was going, though he fully intended on going to Mrs. Diggerty's house. His dick throbbed in his pants, aroused by the dirty talk, but getting no action itself. His breathing was getting a little ragged.

Saks groaned long and loud and panted for a minute. "Goodness gracious, beautiful," he said at last. "You're fucking fantastic."

Luke was on the edge after hearing his friend's orgasm, but there was no good way he could take care of that now. With a start, he realized he was on Mrs. Diggerty's street, and nearly passed her house. He stopped the car suddenly and then backed into the parking space in front of the house. For a few minutes, he put his head on the steering wheel, and then still hearing Saks and the woman stirring in his apartment, pulled the phone out of his pocket and ended the call.

Fucking hell, help me make it through the day, Luke thought. "And I really, *really* need my wife back home," he added out loud.

An hour later, Luke arrived at the hospital and went up the elevators to the maternity floor without asking for permission. They'd have to throw him out to keep him from his wife. He walked into the room, to find Emily crying. "Baby," he said alarmed. "What's wrong? Are you okay? Is the baby okay?"

Emily held out her arms begging for a hug. "No, nothing like that," she snuffled. "I got scared."

Luke wrapped his arms around Emily as best he could. "What the hell happened?"

She buried her head in his arms. "Evan showed up here."

"Evan," said Luke shocked. "What the hell was he doing here?"

"He works here, he said, doing community service. He, he brought me breakfast."

What the fuck? Evan? Here? His hands formed a tight knot in Emily's hair. That was it. He was taking his wife home, doctor or no doctor.

Emily was crying harder now, Luke apparently being no comfort to her.

"He, he said he was going to sue us for getting injured on your property, bankrupt us."

Luke scoffed. "Sweetie, is that what frightened you?" He lifted her head with his fingers and looked into her blue eyes. "Gee," he said with a smile, trying to get her to smile back, "we have bigger problems than that. He'll have to get in line if he wants to do some damage."

Emily swallowed hard. "He thinks that when you get deported, he and I will get back together."

"Baby, baby," said Luke, clutching her tightly. "I'm never going to leave you. I can't. I love you too damn much. I don't care what the government does or what happens down the road. We'll be together."

"I know it," she said, drawing a deep, ragged breath to control her tears. "It's just that he's crazy and I don't know what he'll do next."

Luke wanted to find that jerk and pound him into the ground for upsetting his wife. Of course, that would get Luke arrested and make things worse for him and Emily, but the satisfaction of seeing that man's face bleed was almost worth it. "I won't leave you again despite what the hospital says. They'll have to get security to drag me out of here."

As if to underscore that Luke wasn't supposed to be here this early in the morning, Evelyn swept into the room and then stopped short. She looked Luke up and down.

"This is my husband, Luke," said Emily nervously.

"Nice to meet you, Mr. Wade," said Evelyn, "but you're a little early for visiting hours."

"Who do I make a complaint to?" said Luke.

"Complaint?" said Evelyn.

"Yes, my wife's ex was in here this morning and upset her. There's a restraining order against him."

"What happened?"

"Just that," said Luke.

"He's an orderly here at the hospital," said Emily.

"What's his name?" said Evelyn.

"Evan Waters," replied Luke. His jaw clenched when he said the name.

"Evan, yeah I've seen him around," said Evelyn. "He doesn't seem like a bad guy."

"Believe me, you don't know him. He caused a lot of trouble for my wife and was arrested for it."

"I see," said Evelyn. "I'll make a report to my supervisor and she'll talk to his boss about not coming to your room again. But first things first. Here is some ibuprofen for your headache and something for your blood pressure. Your doctor was called away for an emergency delivery, so the resident will be in to check on you."

"I see," said Emily. Luke watched her spirits sink and he squeezed her hand. "So I'm not going home today."

Evelyn gave a professional smile. "It's up to the doctor, but yours wants some tests done to see how the baby is doing. But that doesn't mean you can't go home today; just not right now. Are you done with this?" She pointed to the uneaten food on Emily's tray.

"Yes. I can't possibly eat it."

Evelyn picked up the cover to the food. "I see what you mean. I'll go zap the eggs a second and get you some fresh toast. I hate soggy toast too. I'll be back in a minute." She left, toting the plate.

"I think that's her middle name."

"What?" said Luke. He was distracted by his thoughts of what punishment he'd like to heap on Evan Waters.

"'I'll be back in minute.' I've never seen a woman move so fast."

A knock sounded on Evelyn's door and Amanda Dougherty stepped in, carrying a paper bag.

"Hi, honey. Hello, Luke." She went to the opposite side of the hospital bed and gave Emily a kiss. "Here; I brought you something."

"What?" said Emily.

"As it happens, I made some donuts."

"Donuts?" said Luke.

"Yeah," said Emily excitedly. "She makes them for... oh, Mom, it's Dad's birthday, isn't it? I forgot all about it."

"Don't worry about it. You've had bigger things on your mind, Emily. But I thought a couple would cheer you up."

"Did you bring cinnamon and sugar?"

"Of course. I know they're your favorite."

"Gimme." She drew one of the donuts out of the bag and broke it in two, handing a piece to Luke. "You've got to try this. There is nothing like a freshly made donut. Oh, Mom," said Emily after she swallowed a bite, "it's wonderful. I haven't had one of these for a long time."

The cake donut was still warm, with cinnamon and sugar clinging tightly to it. Luke had to admit it was delicious, unlike anything from the store or a donut shop.

"How come you never made these for me?" Luke said in mock accusation. "You've been holding out on me, woman."

Emily swallowed another piece of donut.

"Hush, you," said Amanda sternly. "They're a lot of work, even with a good mixer. You need a dough hook, and to raise the dough-like bread, then spread it out and cut out the donuts, and raise them again. That's before you fry them, drain them, and sugar them."

"That's why they're for special occasions," said Emily.

"I'm just teasing her, Mrs. D. But they *are* awesome. Are there any more in that bag?"

"Stop. These are for Emily. Besides, they aren't good for the waistline. If I made them for Sam every time he asked, he'd be as big as a house."

"But I can see the reason now for your long and happy marriage," said Luke with a smile. "That's a potent weapon you have there, Mrs. D."

"My, don't you have the blarney of an Irishman."

Luke supposed it was a natural mistake. Wade could be an Irish name. And Luke at that moment didn't want to explain his ancestry to a woman who treated him coolly. But right then, Evelyn walked in again carrying the plate. She looked over the donut in Emily's hand.

"What is this?" she asked.

"My mom brought me some homemade donuts."

"Homemade?"

"Yes, they have very little salt," said Amanda, "if that's what you are worried about."

"Here, try some," said Emily, pulling out the next donut in the bag.

"That's okay," said Evelyn. "I'm sure they're delicious."

"Yes, they are," said Amanda with a lift of her chin. "And you can see they've done my Emily a world of good. They're downright medicinal."

CHAPTER ELEVEN

New Revelations

"You're a life-saver," Emily told Luke as he handed her the cell phone. She flipped through messages and emails and her Facebook page.

"Anything for you, sweetie," said Luke. Emily's mother had left. She saw that Luke was ready to hang in for the long haul and promised to be back later "with a proper dinner." Emily was grateful for this. For a short space, except for the fact that Emily was in a hospital bed, they were back to their normal roles as husband and wife.

"What on earth did you tell people?" said Emily, alarmed. "People seem to think I'm on the verge of death."

Luke held up his hands. "It wasn't me, I swear. I crashed when I got home last night."

"Must be Angela," Emily huffed. "Look, here it is. It's on her page. 'Just to let you know Emily is doing fine. She's in the hospital overnight but should be home shortly. My big sister will DEFINITELY help me with the wedding.'"

"Just that? No explanation? No wonder people are blowing up your Facebook page."

"I love my sister, but ..."

"Yeah," said Luke. Then he got an idea.

"Give me your phone."

"Why?"

"I want to check something." Emily gave Luke her phone and he scrolled through Angela's extensive friend list.

"What are you doing?"

His gut clenched when he saw what he suspected. "There. Evan's on her friend list. That's how he knew."

"Seriously? I'll have words with her. She should have unfriended him months ago."

"Maybe, but she has over a thousand friends here. With a list like that, how can you keep up?"

A knock on the door interrupted their conversation, and a young doctor entered.

"Hi, Emily. I'm Doctor Emerson, the resident for maternity."

"Hi!" Emily waved and pointed. "This is my husband, Luke."

"Nice to meet you. Emily, I talked with your OBGYN, Doctor Shoo, this morning and we talked about your case. How're you feeling?"

"I'm better." At this point, Emily would say anything to get out of here.

"The nurse reported you had a headache."

"It's better now."

He scrunched his face as he examined her chart. "Still, we don't want to take any chances, so I'm ordering an ultrasound today, and some blood tests. When did you take the blood pressure medicine?"

"An hour ago."

"Well, it takes a while to start working. I'm sure we'll see results by the end of the day. In any case, I expect we'll send you home later and get you set up with some monitoring at home."

"What kind of monitoring?" asked Luke. He stood with his arms crossed, looking over this doctor who couldn't be older than him.

"We have a service where we can weigh Emily, and check her oxygen levels and her blood pressure though equipment we set up in your home. It's just an added precaution and gives us baseline numbers to treat her condition. At twenty-seven weeks, it's just too early to induce labor. We need to get you through another seven weeks at least before we can do that for the baby to be healthy. We'll have to watch you carefully."

"Thirty-four weeks, isn't that too early?" said Emily.

"It's going to depend on how you do, Emily. While we want to keep the baby in you for as long as possible, sometimes it's just better to deliver the baby rather than stress the child and you. Every week longer we can keep the baby in you is better for the baby. But if your health is endangered, that's not good either."

Emily took a deep breath and Luke put his arms around her shoulders. "Is this going to happen again if I have another baby?" asked Emily.

"The odds are against it. Many women who have this condition with their first baby never see it in other pregnancies.

"That's good to know," said Luke. He was trying to keep his tone positive for Emily's sake but his insides churned with worry. "Another baby, eh?" He grinned at her.

"So," said Doctor Emerson, "let's get these tests done, and we'll go from there."

Emily and Luke returned from the ultrasound. Luke had heard the baby's heartbeat. He'd heard it before, but somehow, after everything the past few days, it only made the child that much more real. When the nurse asked if they wanted to know what they were having, he and Emily had both said yes without hesitation. It was then, looking at the fuzzy shapes on the screen that was their baby, that it hit Luke hard.

He was responsible for a new human being.

And then another thought.

"A boy. We're going to have a boy."

The thought thrilled and terrified him.

One part of his brain thought of all the things he'd do with his son, teaching him to ride a bike, baseball games, teaching him how to repair motorcycles. In his mind, he saw the boy growing up. He had Luke's dark hair, but Emily's blue eyes, and maybe he was a little rebellious, like his old man, but he respected his father too. He would love his mother passionately, but complain that she fussed over him too much. He wouldn't keep his room clean, which would annoy his mother, but Luke would understand. When he was a teenager, he'd play his music too loud, which would annoy Luke. But Emily would tell Luke to lighten up on the boy, that Luke had played his music loud too when he was that age. Luke would be terrified the first time his son rode a motorcycle on his own, but proud of him too. When he went to college, Emily would cry, and so would Luke, but not so his wife would see him and tease him about it.

The part the terrified Luke was that he didn't know if he'd measure up as a father. He barely remembered his, and much of that was wrapped around the terror of losing his parents. He didn't stay with any one foster family long enough to know what a father did, and some of them were barely human beings, let alone parents. How could he do this? How could he be a father?

As he walked beside his wife's gurney, he held her hand tightly. Despite his fear that he wouldn't measure up, he felt so much love for her right now he thought his heart would burst. When they got back to her room, when they were alone, he bent over and gave her a kiss. He melted into it just as much as she did, and for a few seconds he felt as if he and she were merged into one being.

"Baby," he breathed when they broke the kiss, "you're so amazing."

She smiled at him with hope and love in her eyes. Luke thought he was the luckiest man on earth to have those eyes shining at him. He had to figure out how to handle all of this quickly, because he couldn't bear it if that beautiful woman looked at him with disappointment in those beautiful blue eyes.

A knock at the door interrupted their sweet moment.

"Hello," said Emily's mother. "Can I come in?"

"Sure, Mom," said Emily. "We just got back from the ultrasound."

"What did you find out?"

At that moment Luke's phone vibrated in his pocket. Taking it out, he saw it was Saks calling. "Yeah," said Luke, turning his back to the women."

"Luke, I'm sorry. I have to close the shop early."

"What's going on?"

"Something came up. Do you want to come by, or should I just lock up?"

Luke's mouth formed a thin line. What was he going to say? He wasn't going to leave Emily, especially not with that jerk, Evan, skulking around. Saks was one argument away from taking off to Florida on his own.

"Anything going on in the shop?"

"I fixed that Suzuki. Otherwise, all I've been doing is playing solitaire on the computer."

"Well, lock it up then. I can't leave Emily."

"Sure, Luke. Sorry, man."

"You can tell me about it later. And you *will* tell me about it later."

Saks sounded hesitant when he spoke. "Sure, Luke. Whatever you say."

Emily watched him with raised eyebrows. "Is there trouble at the shop?"

"Yeah. I have an employee who wants to go to Florida and is looking to provoke me into an argument." He smiled to keep his tone light, his mind still trying to figure out what was going on with Saks.

"Maybe you should lay him off."

"Well, I'm going to have to find a new mechanic anyway to replace Gibs. I'll do that first and break him in over the winter months."

"That sounds like a good plan."

"Luke," said Emily's mother, "I mentioned to Emily that maybe she should come and stay with us a while. You're busy with the shop, and she obviously needs care."

"Mom!" said Emily, exasperated.

"That's very sweet of you, Mrs. D, but I'll take care of Emily. It's my job and I intend to do it."

Amanda Dougherty looked Luke over as if inspecting him for some chink in his armor.

Good, thought Luke. *Let her look. Let her see I'm not letting Emily go anywhere but home.*

Emily's mother sighed. "Well, I suppose I can look in on her from time to time. I'll call Angela and see if she can check her on her way to work."

"That won't be necessary, Mom."

"Actually," said Luke, "that sounds like a good idea. I'll have keys made for you and Angela."

"Luke!" protested Emily.

"Em, I found you passed out on the living room floor. I'm not going to take a chance that I'm not there to make sure you're all right."

"But, baby."

Luke shook his head. "Sweetie, the most important thing is making sure you're safe. And we're going to do that with all hands on deck."

Finally, just before dinner time, the doctor released Emily. All the tests had come back good and her blood pressure seemed to be managed with the prescription. He wrote out a prescription for the blood pressure medicine and instructions that she do no heavy work around the house. Her mother drove home with them and Luke opened the door to let the ladies in. The apartment was filled with the smell of slightly burnt meat, and her mother walked quickly into the kitchen.

"No real harm done. It's good you have one of those crock pots with an automatic shutoff. The food has to be trashed, though." When they got into the apartment, Luke, remembering the impromptu visit from his uncle, called a locksmith to get the locks replaced.

"Is there something wrong?" asked Emily when he got off the phone.

"No. It's just that while we get keys for your sister and mother I thought we'd get some better locks."

Emily gave him a look that said she didn't believe his explanation. "And how much is that going to cost?"

"Don't worry about the cost, baby. You're more important than any amount of money."

Emily opened her mouth as if to argue with him, but the noise of cabinets opening and closing reminded them that Emily's mother was in the house.

"Luke," called her mother, "you definitely need some things here if I'm going to make a decent dinner for you."

"Mom," said Emily. "You don't have to do that. Aren't you and Dad going out for his birthday today?"

"We postponed it till the weekend. You're more important. Besides, he's going to drop by for dinner anyway."

Emily leaned her head back on the couch and mouthed, *shoot me now*.

Luke sat next to her and gave her a hug. "What do you want from the store, Mrs. D? I have to get Emily's medicine from the drugstore."

"I'll make a list."

Luke drew Emily close to him and kissed her hair. She laid his head on his shoulder and sighed.

"It's all so crazy. Luke, how're we going to make it for the next two months?"

Luke didn't know. His stomach clenched with all the things that were going wrong in their life, and he didn't have a clue on how to fix any of it. Maybe he should get that money of his father's tucked away in that off-shore bank and take Emily away somewhere where no one knew them. It was a thought that comforted him briefly, but he knew his wife. As much as she complained about her family, she'd miss them terribly. It would be a stain on their relationship and their marriage if he dragged her away from them. "We're going to make it the way we always do: one step at a time. Hey, ten years apart couldn't tear us down. I doubt anything else will."

Emily kissed his cheek but said nothing. Her blue eyes were filled with worry and he didn't blame her. He was worried too, but he wouldn't add to his wife's upset by showing his own.

"Luke," said Emily's mother as she came into the living room. "Here's that list."

Luke stood and pulled out his wallet. "Use this credit card for the locksmith if he comes before I get home." He put it on the coffee table. "I'll be back as soon as I can."

Giving Emily one last kiss on the cheek, he was out to the door to do his errands.

CHAPTER TWELVE

Betrayal

When Luke got into the truck, the first thing he did was call Matt Stone. The attorney wasn't in, so Luke left a message asking him to call. He got the return call after he finished the shopping at the grocery store, as he stood in the line at the pharmacy. It wasn't the best place to have this conversation. "Thanks for calling. Things have come up." He looked around to see if anyone was listening. It wasn't like Luke to be paranoid, but since his uncle showed up, he was jumpy.

"What's going on?" said Stone.

"First off, there's a woman I want you to call."

"Oh?"

"It's Helen, Gibs' wife. His brother showed up and is looking for part of Gibs' estate."

Stone scoffed. "Really? It always amazes me the way relatives come out of the woodwork after a death. Okay, I'll give her a call. What's her number?"

Luke gave it.

"What else?"

"Evan Waters showed up at the hospital this morning. Emily was very upset. It's not good for her blood pressure."

"Who?"

"Her ex. The one who got her in all that legal trouble."

"Yes, I remember now."

"He told her he was going to sue us for his injuries on our property. He expects to bankrupt me."

"Did you invite him onto the property?"

"No, he came on his own."

"And this was in the fenced-in area off the shop?"

"Yeah, but I don't know if the Rojos dragged him there or not."

"Well, I'll look into that. You've got business insurance, right?"

"Of course. Have to."

"Good to know."

"Anything else?"

"Isn't that enough?"

"Sure, Luke, but for you that's a light day."

Matt was only joking but Luke wasn't in the mood for jokes. He had serious problems and these were the least of them. "There's more to talk about, but I can't here." He almost growled out the response, and his voice came out rough-sounding.

"Okay, when?" Matt's voice got serious, taking a hint from the warning in Luke's voice.

"I'm not sure."

"Can I call you in the morning?"

"Sure, that sounds like a good idea."

"Talk to you then."

Luke paid the co-pay, glad it was relatively cheap medicine, even if it was one that was recommended for pregnant women with Emily's problem. It seemed they were bleeding money everywhere he looked. Even with his insurance, he knew Emily's stay at the hospital was going to cost them. He hadn't thought he'd need the more expensive coverage that takes care of pregnancy, with a low co-pay, and when Emily told him she was pregnant, it was too late to change to policy.

Anything to keep her and the baby healthy, he told himself. Thinking about money seemed wrong at a time like this. Still, his father's money was looking more and more attractive. The only problem was that he'd have to leave the country to get it. And once he left the country, he couldn't get back in for ten years. Damn government red tape. If the government didn't know his father brought him here illegally then things wouldn't be so difficult. But the government had delivered an end run around immigration law by placing Luke's family in the witness protection program.

Maybe it was time to consider that option again, returning to that program. But the problem would still be the same. Emily would be forced to give up her family. And she'd be massively unhappy.

Luke felt like things were closing in around him. If he could just get a few of these monkeys off his back, he and Emily could rest easier.

At least he could relax a bit now that the errands were done and he was on the way home. He hoped the locksmith had gotten there and changed the locks. That would make Luke feel a little better.

He was on the main highway, going past his shop on the way to his apartment complex when he noticed the lights on in his shop. That couldn't be right. Saks said he'd close the shop. Luke thought about the near break-in a few nights ago, and alarm shot through his body.

He swung into the parking lot and slid into the spot at the front door of the garage. Checking it, he found it was locked, but the security system wasn't on. "Damn," Luke cursed, "did Saks forget to set the alarm?"

The lights shouldn't have been on. It raised a red flag. He opened the door and walked in. "Hello!" he called out. But there was no answer. A few steps brought him to the shop entrance of the garage. Here the lights were blazing, but no one was in the large space. There was nothing to hide behind here, but there was the bathroom towards the back. Luke picked up a crowbar he had hanging from the wall and walked to the bathroom. He checked the handle. It wasn't locked. Carefully he unlatched it, and kicked the door in suddenly. The door hit the wall with a thud. He rushed in with a scream, hoping to frighten whoever was there.

But no one was in the bathroom. It was just the one toilet and sink, so nothing was hidden here either.

He walked out of the bathroom, perplexed and feeling slightly foolish.

Still, something was off.

Next to the bathroom door was the entrance to the back garage. It was a solid black door that was usually kept locked because of all the bikes in storage there. Luke turned the handle, and found to his surprise that the door was open. This definitely wasn't right.

Luke pulled open the door to find the lights blazing in that garage too. He scanned the room and didn't see anyone.

But through the large panes of the garage bay doors, he saw a bunch of men in the back parking lot next to the clubhouse. Men wearing Hades' Spawn jackets. Members of his own club. What the hell were they doing here? That back gate was locked for the winter. Then he saw Pepper working a key in the door of the clubhouse.

"What the fuck?" What the hell was Pepper doing? Though officially a member of the Hades' Spawn, Luke didn't expect the DEA agent would dare trespass on his property, especially not after all the shit the DEA had brought down on them. And why were members of the club gathered here without his knowledge?

Luke quickly walked through the garage and opened the single side door to enter the back parking lot. Some of his club brothers snapped their heads up and watched Luke walk toward them.

Henry Spinner, whose club name was Spider, walked to Luke while the others looked on. "Hey, Luke," he said.

"What the fuck's going on, Spider?"

"Luke," he said, spreading out his hands. "We would have told you, but..."

"But? But, what?"

"What," said a gravelly voice behind him, "is that we're taking a vote as to whether you should be kicked out of the Spawn."

Luke whirled to see Okie standing before him.

"Okie? When did you get out?" He looked over at the Spawn's president, fresh from being released from prison, and was glad to see him, but Okie did not have a friendly look on his face.

When Okie spoke, it chilled Luke to the bone.

"None of your damn business. And if what Pepper tells me is true, nothing is going to be your business with Hades' Spawn ever again."

Luke's blood roared in his ears. What the hell did Pepper do now? What did he tell Okie?

"I don't know what you're talking about," hissed Luke, terrified and angry at the same time.

"Come on, Luke," said Pepper, staring him hard in the face. "Those strange men working on the clubhouse when you built it? I did some checking and found the listening equipment."

Luke stared at Pepper in disbelief, and the cold realization hit that Pepper was playing the Spawn again, playing the part of the loyal club member. Only this time, to spin his story he was ratting out Luke. What the hell was he doing? What game was the DEA agent playing now?

He turned to Okie, to the man he loved liked a brother. "Don't do this, Okie. There are things you don't know about."

"So it *is* true. You *are* a snitch."

Fuck! This is what Okie thought of him? Looking around at his club brothers, he saw in their faces that they thought so too. And what did they know? None of these men were at the ill-fated pig roast that turned into a turkey shoot, with the Rojos and the Spawn who were there, being the turkeys. All of them had left the club in disgust when Jack Kinney sported a one-percenter version of the Hades' Spawn patch, announcing the Spawn had joined the ranks of outlaw bikers.

"I told you, Okie," said Pepper, "Things didn't add up about that shootout. Spade walked away clean from it. The government didn't even investigate him."

"Because," Luke yelled, "I was the fucking injured party here, Pepper."

"Just like I told you, Okie. He's lying about everything."

"Okie, man, you know me."

"Yeah, I thought I knew you. But Pepper's not telling me anything that I didn't hear from Lil' Ricki."

"It's not true," denied Luke. He couldn't believe this. The man he'd looked up to and supported when the other club members turned their backs was accusing him of betraying the club?

"I don't think we need a vote now, do we, fellas? He's all but admitted it."

The men murmured their agreement.

"Give me your jacket, Luke," said Okie.

"No."

"I said, boy, give me your fucking jacket or I'll rip it off you. Limbs included."

"Fuck, no."

"Boys," said Okie.

The group of them rushed at Luke and held his arms and shoulders tight as Okie took a knife and cut the stitching of the Hades' Spawn patch on the back of Luke's jacket.

"You're making a mistake!" Luke couldn't believe how much it hurt to be betrayed by his brothers. Physical pain had never hurt this badly.

Okie moved to the front of him and showed him the ripped Hades' Spawn patch. He stared Luke directly in the eye. "I ain't making no mistake, boy. You don't belong in the Hades' Spawn, and perhaps you never did."

Luke swallowed hard. Okie's gaze was fierce and absolute. His judgement was made and there was nothing Luke could do. He shook with anger and at the unfairness of all of this, of all he'd gone through to do what Okie asked him, to keep the club together until he got out of jail. Of the brothers he'd trusted turning his back on him in one the blackest periods of his life. He yelled, "Every single one of you, get off my property! Now!"

"We'll be doing that, and be thankful you're getting off this easy, snitch."

Okie turned away and then turned back again. "On second thought..."

Okie punched Luke so hard in the gut he felt like his insides were splitting in two. He stumbled back a few steps and Okie shot him an evil grin. "Let that be a lesson. We don't tolerate no fuckin' squealers. Let's go!"

With that command, the rest of the Spawn followed Okie through the open gate, Pepper being the last of them. No way was Luke going to let Pepper walk out with a set of keys to his shop.

"Hey, asshole, give me my fucking keys," gasped Luke.

Luke's former employee sighed and tossed the keys to Luke, who barely caught them with one hand while clutching his gut with the other.

"I'm just doing what I have to," said Pepper.

"Fuck you. And don't bother talking to me anymore. I'm not buying."

Pepper nodded and walked through the gate, leaving Luke in the back parking lot of his shop on a cold November afternoon, all alone.

CHAPTER THIRTEEN

The Boss' Order

Emily tried to relax with her feet up on the couch, but her mother buzzing around the apartment didn't make this easy. Her mom seemed to go through every drawer, cabinet, and cupboard.

"Are you looking for something, Mom?" She tried to keep the exasperation out of her voice. She was exhausted and feeling pretty down. She, however, appreciated her mother coming over and cooking for them.

"No. Just checking to see what you need. There's hardly enough room here for all of that. Your apartment's so small." Her mother moved from the kitchen into the hallway and then back into the kitchen, opening the cabinets again. The microwave dinged amongst the noise.

What's she doing now? Emily shook her head and prayed for patience. She was a married woman now, with a baby on the way, but Amanda Dougherty treated her like a child. It was time for change. Emily sat up and forced herself to relax. No more acting like a baby. "What I need, Mom, is for you to talk to me."

"What?" said her mother, sticking her head out from the kitchen.

"Please, just talk to me."

Her mom's eyes opened in surprise. "Well, sure, honey." She walked into the living room carrying two mugs of tea, and handed one to Emily and sat in the side chair beside the sofa. "Tomorrow I'll go to the store and get your cabinets stocked properly."

"You don't have to do that, Mom."

"I want to do that. My little girl needs help and I'm here for you."

Emily looked at her bulging stomach poking up from the throw blanket on it. "Have you looked at me, Mom? You can't call me little."

"Here, do you want a something behind your back? I remember when I was pregnant with both you girls I couldn't do enough to relieve the strain there." Her mother stood and went to the bedroom and brought a pillow from the bed. "Sit forward and I'll just put this—"

"Mom, stop. Just stop. I'm not sick."

"I beg to differ. You have a serious condition."

"Which I'll handle. You can see I'm, well, Luke and I are on top of this."

"You fainted in your apartment. Alone."

"Mom, stuff just happens. I'm fine. The baby's okay. The hospital is minutes away. Please. You stressing over this is not helping me."

Her mother sighed. "You're right, I guess."

Emily looked at her mother, utterly shocked. She'd never heard those words from her.

"You'll find out when you are a parent, that all you want is to make sure that your baby doesn't suffer a moment's discomfort. Of course, you can't stop all of it, but you try, you know?" She played with the hem of her skirt. "I don't want for you to go through what I went through alone. I know you're angry with me for withholding information about your father, your *real* father. But when I married your dad, I promised him I wouldn't. As far as Sam Dougherty was concerned, you were his and he wasn't going to let a man who didn't take responsibility throw a shadow between you two."

Emily stared at her mother, appreciating that she would finally share this with her since she'd found out she had a different biological dad.

"And when you got so stuck on Luke, your dad got scared, perhaps the first time I've seen him afraid. Luke was the wrong sort of boy, for so many reasons, and it crushed your father that you hated him for trying to protect you."

"I had to grow up. Dad wouldn't let me."

"Baby, no matter how old your child is, he or she is always your baby. We'll feel the same way in thirty years, when you're ready to become a grandmother."

Emily bit her lip. Her mother had never been so honest with her. All her life, Emily lived like there was one great big secret that surrounded her. In her bones, she felt she was being lied to. No one wanted to admit it until her mother blurted it out a few months ago. "You know you misjudged Luke when we were in high school."

"Emily, had we met Luke a few months ago instead of ten years ago, we'd still think the same thing. That club of his, those motorcycles! I've only known a couple men with one motorcycle a piece and he has three! Is that where all his money goes?" She shook her head, her judgement clearly written all over her face.

Her mother didn't know. Emily was sure that no matter how much defending of Luke she did, it would never change her parents' minds. They saw the outside, not how good and kind he was inside. "No! As a matter of fact, it costs a lot of money running a business. There're property taxes, payroll, utilities, more taxes, employees, health insurance, supplies—Mom, it takes an incredibly responsible person to handle all that and make a profit. And he did it on his own. If he spent a little money on himself then I don't blame him. Now he's shouldered the expenses for both of us since I can't work. And he's done it without a moment of complaint. So don't you think you can give him some credit? I don't expect Dad to understand. I've accepted he'll never welcome Luke as he's welcomed Justin into the family. But you, Mom? I hope you can see past the club jacket to what a good guy he is."

Her mother opened her mouth to speak, but just then a knock at the door interrupted, or, by the look on her face, saved her. "I'll get that," she said a little too eagerly. "It must be the locksmith."

Emily settled back into the couch with a sigh. She was fighting an uphill battle with her mother regarding Luke, and she might as well accept it. She felt the rush of cold November air when her mother opened the door.

"No, he's not here," said her mother. Her voice was strained, as if she was upset.

Emily sat up and looked over the top of the couch. She couldn't see who was at the door. "Mom, who is that?"

"I'm Robert Gibson, ma'am. I'm, I was, Frank Gibson's brother.

"Mom, show him in."

"Emily, I don't think..."

"Sure, I'm happy to come in."

Emily heard her mother whisper something, but she couldn't hear all the words.

"And the shut the door, please, Mom. It's getting cold in here. Can we get you anything, Mr. Gibson, coffee or tea?"

"No, I won't be staying long. I wanted to talk to Luke about Frank's bike."

Emily raised her eyebrows when she saw Gibs' brother as he came into the living area. He was almost the spitting image of Luke's friend and employee. "I can tell you two were brothers."

"Yes, ma'am. Everyone always says so. And if you don't mind me saying so, you are a beautiful woman. Luke's a lucky guy."

Emily smiled. "Thanks. I tell him that all the time. And you don't have to call me ma'am. That makes me sound old. Please, call me Emily."

Rob smiled warmly at her, showing his chipped front teeth. "I met Luke at the hospital when you were in the ER. I hope you're doing okay."

"Well, Junior here wants to give his mom a hard time, but we'll be fine." Emily smiled. Why hadn't Luke told her about Rob?

"That's good to hear," said Rob. He glanced around the apartment. "This is a nice place you have here."

For a reason she could not place, maybe because he seemed so much like Gibs, maybe because he seemed so friendly, Emily warmed to the stranger in her living room, despite the look on her mother's face. "Thanks. We're hoping to be getting a bigger place soon. This is only a one-bedroom."

"Oh? Thinking of buying a house?"

Emily shrugged. "We'll see."

"A house is always good. Gives the kid a place to run around."

"That's very nice," said her mother coldly. "But Emily needs her rest, *Mr.* Gibson."

He looked at her mother, and Emily noticed his face grow sad. What was that about? Maybe he just wanted to talk about his brother. "Mom, you're being rude."

"No, that's okay," said Rob. "Your mother's right. I'll come back another time and talk to Luke about that bike. But, uh, do you mind if I use your bathroom? My hotel's across town."

Her mother glared openly at Gibs' brother. Emily shook her head as she sat forward on the couch. "Go through the bedroom," said Emily. "It's on the left." She gave her mother a *what-the-hell* look.

"Thanks," said Rob.

When he left the room, Emily turned to her mother. "What was that about?" she said in a low voice.

"Emily, you don't know that man. He practically barged in here."

"I've never known you to be rude to anyone."

"There's always a first time," said her mother, looking away and crossing her arms.

Why on earth would she treat a stranger so poorly? This was so out of character for Amanda Dougherty. Emily couldn't fathom it. Maybe Luke had said something to her mother? Should she be worried?

The toilet flushed and Rob came back into the living room.

"It was nice to meet you, Emily. Like I said, I'll be back."

"I'll show you to the door," said her mother, tightly.

"Thanks," said Rob.

After a few moments, the cold continued to flush into the room and Emily began to wonder what was going on. Maybe staying in the hospital would have been a better idea. Everything seemed jacked up and upside-down these days.

"Emily, the locksmith's here."

"Oh, good." She shivered. "Are you able to shut the door?"

"He says it won't take long. Let me get you another blanket."

Twenty minutes later, the heat in the apartment cranked continually as the locksmith opened and shut the door as he worked. Emily shivered under her blanket and her mother ended up having to put on her coat.

Even though her mother brought more tea, it barely warmed her. She turned on the TV, something she rarely did. Her mother kept pacing about the apartment, and it began to get on Emily's nerves. She seemed oddly nervous for having a locksmith fixing the door.

"Okay, ma'am," said the locksmith. "I've got you set up with a new lock and a deadbolt and a peephole, as the mister asked. There's an additional charge for the extra keys, and I've got to go to my truck to make them. But here's the bill."

Emily got up and waddled over to him, handing him the credit card. "This should take care of it."

True to the cyber age, the locksmith bought out his smart phone and swiped the card. "If you give me your email address, I'll send you the receipt."

"Sure." Emily gave him the email address for the bike shop.

"Great. Everything's good. I'll be back in a couple minutes with the keys. Promise. It's too cold out there to stay out too long."

"I appreciate everything you've done."

"I'm so glad that the locks are done," her mom commented as the man left. She continued pacing the living room.

"Mom." It wasn't a question.

"What?"

"What the hell's going on? You're acting like a caged animal."

"I guess I'm keyed up," replied her mother. "You being in the hospital and everything. Are you sure you shouldn't have stayed?"

"Mom, please. I couldn't have stayed there another minute. Just being in the hospital made me feel sick." She didn't mention being home didn't seem to be helping either at the moment.

"Where's that husband of yours?" Amanda said, exasperated. "Dinner's going to be late."

"Mom, please. Relax. You're stressing me out."

There was another knock on the door.

"Is it always like this?" said her mother. "No wonder your blood pressure is through the roof."

"For shit's sake," said Emily rubbing her eyes. "It's probably the locksmith returning with the keys."

Her mother moved to the door again. Opening it brought another rush of chilly air. "Who are you? You can't come in here!"

Emily turned to watch a couple of rough-looking Hispanics push her mother against the wall and barge into the apartment.

"What the hell!" Emily's heart jack-hammered in her chest. In a moment of lucidity, Emily pulled out her cell phone and tried to dial 911, but her hands were shaking too hard from cold and fear.

"That's her," one of the men said gruffly, his accent thick.

Emily clutched the phone under her blanket.

A second man reached inside his jacket and pulled out a gun, holding it against her mother's head; the other advanced on Emily.

"Get out of my house!" she screamed.

"Get up," said the man, coming at her. He wore a leather jacket, though at this point Emily couldn't see the patch. He wore some black diamonds on the front, which Emily knew was not a good sign. These men were not just criminals, they were dangerous criminals.

"Leave my daughter alone!" cried her mother, frozen against the wall as the gun pressed against her temple. "Please. Can't you see she's pregnant?"

"Yeah, we know," the larger, big bellied man barked. "Get up or my friend here won't hesitate to put a bullet in your mama's head."

Emily struggled to get up, scooping her phone as she did so and slipping it in her pocket.

"You, mama, get her coat. She's going on a little trip."

"Where?" Her mother had been a nervous wreck a moment ago with a locksmith, and now she was tough as a bear protecting her cubs.

"Shut the fuck up!" The guy close to her pressed the barrel of the gun harder against the side of her head. "Coat! Now!"

"Please, Mom. Just grab my coat." Emily felt the hot tears sting as they ran down her face. Where was Luke? Had these men come after him first?

Her mother, visibly trembling, got Emily's coat from the closet. Big-belly ripped it from her hands. He swung around to Emily and glared at her, as if begging for an excuse to hit her. "Put that on! Now! Or your *mamacita* gets it."

Emily struggled to get her coat on and do it up. It had grown tight over her belly. *Please little one, stay safe inside me.*

"Let's go. The Boss is waiting."

"What about her?" said the other, pointing at Emily's mother.

"You know what to do."

"No!" yelled Emily. "Don't hurt her!"

"No one's getting hurt, little mama—yet. It's not on the order. However, you need to move, snap! The boss is waiting on ya and he hates to be kept waiting."

CHAPTER FOURTEEN

Aftermath

Luke stood alone in the back parking lot of his shop, shocked, not knowing what to do next. He couldn't believe Okie had stripped his patch from him, especially on the say-so of Pepper. Okie didn't know that Pepper was a DEA agent and Luke was sworn to secrecy. He scrubbed his face with his hands, stunned by the actions of his club's president and the utter backing of them by people he thought of as brothers and friends.

It was unfathomable.

A crunch of boots on gravel caused Luke to whip around.

"Hey, Luke."

Luke stared at Saks, who was wearing a dark wool coat, not his usual club jacket. Why was he here? Why wasn't he wearing his Spawn colors? "Did you know?"

Saks shrugged. "I didn't think it was right, so I handed in my jacket."

Luke stared at him in surprise, shocked, and, in a strange sense, honored that Saks stuck up for him against the Hades' Spawn. He then grew angry that they pushed Saks that far or accepted the resignation. He didn't know what was wrong with Okie, but Saks deserved more from the club than an easy out. "You shouldn't have done it."

"Any club that would turn on someone like you? Not worth the effort. Besides, my family's been after me to quit the club anyway. Conflict of interests."

"I thought you weren't involved in the family business."

"I'm not. But since that tussle with the Rojos in August, they've been eyeing the club with suspicion."

"That's on Jack Kinney."

"They know who did what and why. But they don't trust that the DEA was all in the shit of the club."

"How did you know about that?"

"There's a reason that family is on the force, Luke."

Luke thought about how Saks' cousin, Detective Anglotti, leaned on him and Emily, going so far as to execute a search warrant for both his home and his business.

"Shit," said Luke. "Your cousin gave me a hell of a time."

"Yeah. For my part, I'm sincerely sorry about that. And we couldn't shake that asshole Pepper's tree. He's good. I'll give him that. But there're certain members of my family who would kill him rather than look at him, so he'd better not get in their way."

"I thought wise-guys were legit businessmen now."

Saks chuckled. "There's spin on every carousel. Come on, let's get a beer."

The thought was tempting. The stinging rejection by the Spawn made Luke want to lick his wounds, but his wife and her mother was waiting on him for the groceries.

"No, I have to get home to Emily. She must be wondering if something happened to me."

"Well, something did."

Saks' phone rang, and he turned his back to Luke to answer it. "Fuck! No. You think? No, I'm right here with him. Yeah. See you in a few." Saks spun to face him. "Luke, you need to keep your shit together, man," his voice dropped to a level of alarm as he stared at Luke, fear now in his eyes.

Cold dread washed over Luke. "What? What the hell happened?" His thoughts went straight to Emily.

"Promise you're going to keep your shit together." Saks' tone was urgent, and it frightened the crap out of Luke.

"Yeah, just tell me what the fuck's going on."

"This locksmith at your apartment stepped away for a few minutes to make some keys. When he returned, your mother-in-law was unconscious on the floor."

"I've got to get home," said Luke, his panic rising. He started moving toward his truck.

Saks grabbed him arm. "Wait, Luke. There's more."

Luke swallowed hard. "Emily," he whispered. "Is she okay?"

"He doesn't know, Luke. Emily's missing."

"What?" Luke took a step back. "What?" He blinked, and his heart hammered against his chest as a fear he hadn't felt since he was a child flowed through him. "Who the hell did this?" His voice was cold as ice.

"I don't know." Saks pulled his arm. "Come on. Let's go. I'll drive."

They left Saks' winter rat of a beater car at the shop after Saks raced through and turned the lights off. Luke made sure every door was locked, though his hands were shaking as he did. Every instinct told him to get home as fast as he could and every second he couldn't stole minutes from his life. *Possibly Emily's life. And our baby's.*

Luke could barely see the road in front of him. His vision bounced as his fear gripped him. His focus cleared as he tried to calm his breathing. It was a good thing Saks was driving because Luke was sure he'd have an accident trying to tear his way home.

Saks was on the phone with his headset in place, calling out names to his phone to call, and then leaving urgent messages or having terse conversations.

"Yeah, tell Uncle Vits we need to know who did this. Who? Candidates are the Hombres or the Rojos."

"Or," said Luke quietly, "her ex, Evan Waters."

"Hold on, Luigi. What Luke?"

"Evan Waters. We've had restraining orders on him. He doesn't leave her alone."

"Okay, Luigi, there's this dick, Evan Waters, who's been bothering her. You know about him? Okay then."

"And," said Luke, letting a shiver of a sigh escape his lips, "my uncle." He couldn't deny that his uncle could be a part of this. With his crazy insistence that Luke go to Mexico to help run the family drug business, it made him a likely suspect.

"Hold on, Luigi." Saks looked at Luke. "What uncle? I thought you didn't have any family?"

My uncle, Raymondo Icherra. He came to my apartment. Said I should come to Mexico. He also said that I needed some convincing. I didn't pay much attention at the time. I didn't think he'd do anything like this.

"Icherra? As in the Mexican drug lord? What, Luigi? You know about this guy too? The family is in talks with him? Damn. No one keeps me in the loop. Find out what you can Luigi. This is getting worse by the minute."

Luke slammed his fists on his thighs. "She's in a high-risk pregnancy and shouldn't have any stress. If anything happens to her or my son, there's going to be hell to pay."

"Keep your shit together, Luke. We're going to find out who has her. And we're going to get her."

"We?"

"Yeah. I'm calling in the troops on this one. No one is going to mess with my boss. Or my friend."

"I can't ask you to do that, Saks."

"You can't stop me, Luke. Listen. Here's what you don't know about me. My mom made my dad promise to keep me out of the family business. To keep my mom happy, he agreed, but it's been tough, you know? I'm always the odd man out. People don't talk to me at family functions much. I'm always coming into conversations where people stop talking."

Luke wondered if Saks' was talking because he needed to or just to distract Luke as they drove.

Saks shook his head. "College wasn't exactly my thing, and the only thing I really liked was motorcycles. I worked shit jobs to get the money together for the Harley school. But even after that there were few shops willing to give an inexperienced guy a job. Until you. And while you didn't sponsor me into the Spawn because you were too new yourself, you paved the way for me. For the first time, I had a place where I could be myself and the conversations didn't stop when I came into the room."

Luke gave a terse smile. "Hell, Saks. I've seen guys with experience who couldn't break an engine down and put it together like you."

"Still, you took a chance on me. I know I play it on the down-low, but you're like the brother I never had."

Luke didn't know what to say. In the Spawn, they all said they were brothers. By and large, the guys did stand by each other, at least until today. Saks was always a good employee and didn't complain about things much. They enjoyed hanging out at club functions, and on road trips, but he had no idea that Saks felt that way about him. This only showed how close to the vest Saks played things. Heck, Luke didn't even know Saks' family was wise guys until last August.

And now the guy went and quit the club for Luke's sake.

You couldn't buy that kind of loyalty.

They were almost at Luke's apartment building, and right away Luke could tell there was a commotion. Police cars sat in the parking lot with their lights strobing, and his neighbors stood on their balconies in the sharp cold, straining to get a look at what was going on.

"Good," said Saks. "Luigi's here."

Luke remembered this name from Saks' phone conversation. "Who's Luigi?"

Saks smiled grimly. "You know him as Detective Anglotti."

"Luigi is his first name? Like in the video game?"

"Yeah. At the station he uses Louis, but his birth name is Luigi. I used to tease him about it all the time. Might be why he's got that chip on his shoulder when it comes to me. Where's your parking space?"

Saks swung into the parking lot of Luke's building where an ambulance and police cars were parked at the entrance of the walkways. After parking in Luke's space they both rushed over, only to be stopped by a uniformed officer.

"This is a crime scene," the officer announced.

Anglotti walked to them "That's okay, Stevens, this is the husband of the victim." He glared at Saks. "What are you doing here?"

"Making sure Luke gets home without crashing his truck."

"Well, you can go now."

"Can't. Left my vehicle at the shop. I'll just stick around."

"Then stay out of my way. Mr. Wade, I need to ask you some questions."

"Sure, in a minute. Where's my mother-in-law?"

Anglotti pointed to the ambulance. "She's there. But she refuses to be transported."

"Does she need to be?"

"She took a blow to the head and should be checked out."

"Right."

Luke made his way to the ambulance where Amanda had a blanket over her shoulder and a paramedic taking her blood pressure. A bandage was over her right eye, though blood bled through.

"Mrs. D, what happened?"

"They took her, Luke."

"Who?"

"Two Hispanic men. I don't know why."

"Oh for heaven's sake! I'm her husband!"

Sam Dougherty pushed through the police and almost ran to the ambulance, pushing Luke aside roughly when he got there.

"Amanda, are you all right? What the hell happened here? Where's Emily?"

"If you don't mind, sir," said the paramedic, "I'm trying to get her vitals. Her heart rate is fast. With that blow to the head she really needs to be looked at in the Emergency Room."

"Of course. Take her."

"Sam," said Amanda in appeal.

"No buts about it, Amanda. I'll be right after you, as soon as I find out what happened."

"Okay, Sam," said Amanda with resignation, and she allowed the paramedic to bring her into the back of the truck and close the doors. As soon as they were shut fast, Sam Dougherty turned and rushed Luke, grabbing his jacket with both hands.

"What the fuck happened here?"

Luke stood stock-still, surprised and shocked that Sam laid hands on him. Luke quelled the instinct to react. This man was his father-in-law, and only bad things would come out of the two men exchanging blows.

It was Anglotti who stepped forward and pulled on Sam's arm. "Sir, I'm Detective Anglotti. Step away from Mr. Wade."

"This asshole has been nothing but trouble," spit Sam. "Do you see what your criminal activities have brought on us?"

"Sir, Mr. Wade is not being charged with any crime."

"You know what happened with that club of his."

"Yes, and the men involved in criminal activities are under arrest and awaiting prosecution. I can tell you with certainty that Mr. Wade was not involved in their activities. He has been investigated and cleared by our investigations."

Sam glowered at Luke. "I know you're responsible for this." He pushed Luke away with a hard shove.

Luke stared at Sam, his jaw clenched tight, cold anger washing through him. It was possible. If his uncle was behind this, then he was responsible for Emily getting kidnapped.

"Now, what is your relation to Mr. Wade here?" said Anglotti.

"He's my daughter's husband."

Yeah, thought Luke. *Not son-in-law. Never that.*

"Your daughter being Emily Wade?"

"Yes."

"Sir, we regret to inform you that your wife, Amanda Dougherty, has reported to us that Emily was kidnapped by persons unknown. We are currently investigating this crime. Do you have any knowledge of the events of this day?"

"I was coming here for dinner with my wife, Emily, and this asshole." He jerked his thumb at Luke. "And found this."

"Sir, since you have no other knowledge of today's events, I'm going to ask you to leave the crime scene. We'll be in touch if we have any questions."

"Fine. I have to get to the hospital anyway." With a final hard stare at Luke, he turned and walked to his car.

Luke let out a small sigh of relief that Sam Dougherty was now gone.

Anglotti swung to face him with a notepad in his hand. "Now, tell me everything you know about who might have kidnapped your wife."

CHAPTER FIFTEEN

Kidnapped

Emily rode blindfolded in the back of a car. That's all she knew. She had no idea who took her or where she was going or what they were going to do. At least being blindfolded might be a good thing. She remembered from crime shows that if the criminals didn't expect to return you they wouldn't blindfold you.

She shivered, cold, deeply frightened, and missing the strong arms of her husband. She focused on breathing, trying to stay calm for the sake of the baby, knowing if she got too anxious her blood pressure would soar and could cause more problems.

The baby kicked furiously, as if agreeing with her.

At least she had the use of her hands. The first thing she did was fiddle with her phone's audio to turn it off. This was another thing she remembered from crime shows, that a cell phone always rang at the wrong time. She had to think hard about which button was which, but apparently she had nothing but time. The drive seemed to last forever.

She was exhausted. Her heart pounded in her chest and her ears rang. She hoped she would be okay on so many different levels—her health *and* her safety. Why were they after her anyway? If this had something to do with Evan, she was going to kill him with her bare hands. She'd have this baby in prison if she had to. "Please, God. Let me stay okay for the baby."

It was all too much. Why was she kidnapped? Who would do this? Why were they driving such a long time? She couldn't help it. Emily couldn't keep her eyes opened any more. Her exhaustion took hold and the warmth of the car lulled her to sleep. She felt her head fall slowly against the cool window.

"Baby, what's wrong?"

She found herself in the same field as a previous dream. Luke sat next to her on the soft grass. The sun was setting, but the air was still warm.

"Baby," said Emily. "I don't know where I am."

"It's okay. You're here." Luke took her hand and pressed it to his heart.

"I'm frightened. I want to go home."

"I know, sweetheart. You have to stay strong. It's not just us anymore." He placed his hand on her stomach. "He needs us to be strong."

Her eyes jerked open as the car lurched to a stop. The door opened, and a hand touched her arm. "Come on, now."

"Where are we?" She felt desperate, that, if she went where this unseen man wanted, she was walking further away from her life.

"It's better if you don't know. I'll hold your arm. You just follow." It was silly to think this, but the man's voice and manner was almost kind. But he was a kidnapper, holding her against her will.

"I want to go home."

He pulled her arm harder. "You should know by now that's not happening. Come on. It's fucking cold out here and I want to get inside."

The cold was no lie. An icy breeze whipped up, causing her to shudder. Emily couldn't feel the sun on her. It must be night by now.

The man was pulling her harder now, and she had to follow or she would stumble. She couldn't image how much more a fall would screw her up, so she did her best to follow. When she stumbled on uneven pavement, the man kept her upright. He stopped and a rush of warm air greeted her.

"Inside," he said. Once again he led her, though this time she felt warmth close around her and the sounds of being outside, traffic, birds, and wind, were shut out. The floor under here was even and felt carpeted. Doors opened and closed, though those sounded far away. A card sliding home and a beep confirmed that she was in a hotel.

She was led across more carpet.

"Here," he said, "is the bed. Put your feet up. The doctor will be here in a few minutes."

Alarm shot through Emily. What would they have a doctor do?

"Don't harm my baby," gasped Emily.

"Keep that blindfold on," the man said roughly.

"You're not taking my baby!" she shouted as the door shut, and she had a feeling she was alone. Emily tore off the mask and found the room in total darkness. She reached around, trying to find something, anything to help her. She fumbled for the light on the table she felt near the bed, but it wouldn't turn on. She briefly considered moving around the room to find a light switch, but she couldn't see anything and was afraid she'd trip and fall. Feeling around the table for a telephone, she rejoiced when her hands reached it, but deflated just as quickly when there was no dial tone.

Though she didn't like it, she was forced to sit on the bed and wait.

Fear caused her heart to race, and her nerves formed a sickening knot in the hollow of her stomach. She hadn't eaten since breakfast, feasting on her mother's doughnuts, but now her stomach grumbled and she felt lightheaded.

This was not good.

She heard fumbling at the door and quickly put the blindfold back on. She didn't want to lower her chances of going home by seeing something or someone she shouldn't. *Please, Lord. Let someone pick up on my cell phone signal.*

A light switch flicked and the edges of her blindfold were filled with a bright glow.

"Good. You know how to follow instructions."

Emily gritted her teeth. The last thing she wanted was to follow any of these animal's instructions.

"The doctor here is going to look you over. Cooperate and I'll get you something to eat.

Emily's stomach grumbled, but the last thing she wanted was to eat anything this criminal gave her.

A blood pressure cuff was looped over her arm, and she felt the squeeze as the doctor pressed a stethoscope to the inside of her elbow and pumped up the cuff. He grunted as he took the stethoscope away from her arm.

"Your blood pressure is high."

"What do you expect?" spit Emily. "You kidnapped me from my own home!"

"Your heart rate is high."

"What don't you understand about being kidnapped?"

"I'm giving you some Demerol to calm you. I can't have you stroking out."

"Take me home and I'll be fine."

"Sorry. That's not on the menu."

Emily didn't like the man's unprofessional tone. What kind of 'doctor' could this be? Not someone who had a respectable practice or worked in a hospital. She didn't trust him or anything he wanted to do to her. "I'm not taking any of your drugs."

"Sweetheart, you need 'em. You don't want to stroke out, do you?"

"No," said Emily, her voice trembling. "But I don't want anything that would hurt my baby either."

"A little Demerol won't hurt your child. And after that I'll give you the blood pressure medicine you should have. You're high-risk Emily, which is why the boss hired me."

"Who's this boss," spit Emily angrily. "I want to talk to him."

"You will," said the other man in the room. "He has some business to take care of, but he'll be here soon. And then we can get going."

"Quiet, asshole. Don't upset her any more than she is."

"Where are we going?" said Emily.

He held her arm down and she flinched from a pinch. "Somewhere safe."

"Safe would be anywhere but here..." The room began to spin. This wasn't like the medicine they gave her at the hospital. Emily lapsed in and out of wakefulness. Time became meaningless. The door opened and closed many times.

"Why isn't she awake?"

"She fine, just reacted a little more strongly than—"

"Unacceptable. You're supposed to know what you're doing."

"I do. Everyone's different. Her blood pressure has come down. That's why I gave her the medicine."

Emily heard herself moan and tried to cover her mouth. Who were these people? What did they want? This was bad. So dangerously bad. She needed to be home. "Luke," she murmured.

"What did she say?"

"Luke. She keeps calling his name."

"That's her husband."

"I have to go home," she muttered and tried to roll over. "The stew's burning."

"What the hell's she muttering about? Is she okay? The boss wants her and the baby in one piece."

Who was this 'boss' they kept talking about?

A moment of lucidity washed over Emily when they mentioned the baby. What did they want with him? They weren't going to take him, were they? "Don't hurt my baby. I'll rip your hearts out if you try."

Someone laughed. "No one's going to hurt your baby."

It was all too much. The room spun again, and men she didn't know wouldn't let her go home. Her cheeks were wet, and she brought her hands to her face to wipe it away. But it kept coming, and she realized she was crying.

"You've upset her," said one man roughly. Emily thought it might be the voice of the doctor.

"It's your job to keep her calm."

"Then get the fuck out of here."

"Here," said the other man, rattling a paper bag. "I brought some food."

"Yeah, great. Greasy burgers and fries. Wonderful stuff for a pregnant woman. Is there anything to drink? She shouldn't have the salt. I've seen her medical report."

"I'll get something to drink."

"Good. Make sure at least one of them doesn't have any caffeine. In fact, bring some bottles of cold water."

"Right."

A strong arm went around Emily's shoulder and she tried to jerk away. The strong arm stayed. "Here, let me help you sit up."

"Leave me alone."

"Don't be like that. You must be hungry and you need to eat."

"I don't want to."

"For your baby. You have to eat for your baby."

Emily did her best to sit, and the doctor helped her. It was difficult because her swollen belly made sitting up from lying down difficult. Even with help, she felt like a beached whale.

"Here, I put a couple more pillows in back of you. Now you can sit."

"Sure," murmured Emily.

"Try this." Emily's nose wrinkled at the smell of greasy bread and meat.

"It smells awful," she said as she gagged.

"Try a little. Here, I'll break off a small bit. Take this." He held some of the burger to her lips and she took it in. It smelled worse than it tasted. "That's good," encouraged the doctor as he continued to feed her like she was a small bird. "We'll get you something better for breakfast."

Dear God, please let Luke find me soon, Emily prayed. She hoped it was one prayer that would be answered.

CHAPTER SIXTEEN

A Secret Shared

Evan Waters was wild-eyed when Anglotti questioned him. "What the hell are you talking about?"

Luke stared at Emily's old boyfriend through the glass, with his arms crossed. He wanted to break that glass down and hop over and pound that arrogant jerk's face in. But he also knew that he was here on sufferance, a special privilege granted by Anglotti, so he needed to remain calm. His phone buzzed in his pocket. Drawing it out, he didn't recognize the number.

"Hello, Luke here."

"This is Sam. Sam Dougherty. I got your number from Angela."

This was a surprise.

Emily's father's voice was different somehow. Chastened maybe, or just more quiet. Perhaps it was because he was still at the hospital. Luke heard the background noises of announcements and beeps you'd hear in an institutional setting.

This was a surprise.

"How is Mrs. D?"

"She's shaken, but she'll be fine. Listen, Luke. I have to tell you something." The man became quiet, long enough so Luke thought the call dropped, but the counter for the length of time ticked on.

"Mr. D?"

"Yes, I'm still here. Someone came by the apartment today while you were gone."

"Yeah?"

"I think, given his history, maybe the police should look into him."

"Who?" said Luke. He was trying to remain calm, but, given the circumstances, he was ready to blow like a rocket at any minute.

"Rob Gibson. He said he came by to discuss your deceased employee's bike, but I don't think so."

"Why is that, Mr. D?" Luke tried hard to stay calm to make sense of everything. How had everything gotten so fucked up? Why was Rob Gibson at his apartment? Luke tapped the tip of his boot against the floor, waiting for Sam Dougherty's achingly slow answer.

"You have to understand that when we knew him in high school, he wasn't particularly stable. He was always in trouble, not like his brother. Little stuff, you know, but—"

"Why do you think the police should investigate him? He has nothing to do with Emily."

"Yes. He does." There was another long silence. "He's Emily's father." The last words were so choked that Luke could barely make them out. But when he realized what Sam Dougherty had said, shock washed over Luke.

Gibs' brother was Emily's father? The jerk who was bothering Helen?

One of the things that upset Emily about Sam was that he refused to discuss her biological father with her. That and his treatment of her, like she was a loose cannon ready to go off, created a wide gulf between father and daughter.

"What do you mean he wasn't particularly stable?"

"Amanda tried to talk to him for weeks, but he kept pushing her off, or wouldn't take her calls. She cornered him at prom, but he ran off when she told him."

"And he never tried to get in touch with her, or Emily, in all this time?"

"He called once, on Emily's first birthday, after we were married, but I hung up on him. Not since then. No."

"And he showed up at my apartment today?"

"That's what Amanda said. She's very upset about it."

"I can imagine. Does Emily know?"

"About Rob? No. And I'd appreciate it if you didn't tell her."

Luke bit back the remark that came to mind—that he couldn't tell Emily anything, not while she was missing. "I can't make any promises about that, Sam. She's my wife, and we don't keep things from each other."

Sam Dougherty sighed loud enough for Luke to hear. "Yes, I guess you're right. Secrets only seem to hurt."

Luke was glad that Sam realized that, but that wasn't going to help find Emily. A little too late. "Okay. Thanks for telling me. I'll tell the police. They might call you."

"That's fine. Anything to help bring my girl back home."

My girl. What could Luke say to that? "Bye, Mr. D." Luke hung up the phone and shook his head. Clearly Sam Dougherty loved Emily, the daughter of another, yet claimed as his own. It was too bad that, in trying to protect her from the wrongs done to her by her biological father, Sam Dougherty created a rift between him and Emily.

How would he feel if his own child turned him away like Emily did to the man who raised her? There were no easy answers to that and in the end Luke had no say about that issue. Still, when he got Emily back he'd let her know how torn up her father was that she was missing.

Still the question remained. Was Rob Gibson responsible for Emily's kidnapping? He didn't know enough about the man to say.

"Fuck you!" screamed Evan.

Luke's eyes snapped back to the mirror. Anglotti leaned aggressively over the table that separated him and Evan. Waters leaned away with his head turned to the side.

"I have nothing to do with this! I've been working. Two jobs, yeah. So even if I wanted to kidnap Emily, I wouldn't have the fucking time."

He turned his head to stare at Anglotti. "So, asshole, either charge me and call my lawyer, or let me the hell out of here."

Anglotti walked out of the interview room, and Luke moved to meet him in the hall.

"Well, he's good and worked up," said Anglotti with a sneer. "But I don't think he has anything to do with this. I'll let him sit in the tank to calm down."

"What makes you think he didn't take Emily?"

"You heard him. He was surprised to hear she was gone. And then he blamed you for not taking care of her."

No. Luke did not hear him. He was too busy talking to Emily's father. "What a prince," said Luke. "And what about Icherra?"

"We're still looking for him."

"The police?" asked Luke, cocking an eyebrow.

"No. Not just the police. My uncle was beside himself to hear about this whole thing. He's got the crew keeping an eye out."

A door open and closed at the end of the hall and two men walked toward them, their footfalls clicking on the lime green linoleum. One was an older middle-aged man, with a beer gut that wasn't concealed by his suit jacket, and the other a man who appeared to be in his thirties, with medium brown hair and brown eyes. His dark gray suit and dark blue tie seemed to clash with his complexion.

"Fuck," said Anglotti under his breath. He pulled his head up and smiled. "What's up, Captain?"

The older man turned to the other standing with him. "This is Special Agent Randolph Webb. He's assigned to the Wade case."

"That was quick," said Anglotti, extending his hand. "Lou Anglotti, and this is Luke Wade, the victim's husband."

Webb's eyes swept over Luke, his expression cool and unreadable. "Wade? I thought his name was Icherra."

"There's a story to that," said Anglotti. "But the community here has known him as Luke Wade since he was a child."

"You were questioning him." *This is bullshit! Who does this ass-hat think he is?* Luke was tired of being talked about like he wasn't there, but he reminded himself he was there only with his promise to keep his cool. This was getting very difficult, especially since his level of anxiety was rising every minute they didn't find Emily. He wanted to find his wife; who gave a fuck about anything else?

"Mr. Wade gave his statement."

"I see," said Webb. "I'm here as an advance man. The FBI team on kidnappings will be here as soon as we can bring them in. We'll have to set up a base at your house, Mr. Wade."

"I have an apartment."

"And do you have a landline?"

"No. We each have our smart phones. No need for a landline. I do have a landline at my business."

"And does your wife have her phone on her?"

"I'm not sure. When all this happened I wasn't allowed into my apartment, so I couldn't see if it was there."

"I see. Is there an inventory of the crime scene? Let's check to see if a phone was there."

The man was sure fond of saying 'I see,' Luke thought. It also didn't escape him how quickly the man took over the situation.

"And have you interrogated anyone else?"

"We have Mrs. Wade's ex-boyfriend in custody. He doesn't seem to know anything, though he just asked for a lawyer."

Webb's eyes narrowed. "Where is he now?"

"In the interrogation room."

"Keep him there and get me that inventory. Thank you, Captain. I'm sure I can take it from here. Mr. Wade, can I have a few words with you?"

Bang, bang, bang. Webb had everyone hopping to his tune. Anglotti opened another interrogation room and Webb pointed the way to Luke. Reluctantly, Luke entered and then turned to Webb.

The agent looked at Luke and stared at him like he was a subject. The seconds ticked away and Luke realized with a sour chuckle that this was this man's method of unsettling a person he planned on interrogating.

"You've got something to say, Agent Webb, say it."

Webb's nostrils flared. Luke didn't take his eyes off him. "I've got a very thick file on you, Icherra. I've done nothing but read it on my way in from Washington."

"Washington, eh? So I get the A-team?"

"You're fucking right you got the A- team, Icherra. Just your uncle alone ticks that box. What I want to know is what your part is in all of this."

"My part? What the fuck do you think my part is? My wife was kidnapped! Out of our home, damn it!"

"It's unlikely that Emily Rose Dougherty, Miss-girl-next-door-who-never-did-any-wrong, did anything to deserve that, Mr. Icherra. Yes, I read up on her too. Her file's very thin. Aside from some trouble earlier in the year, the girl is as squeaky clean as a bathtub toy. No, her trouble started when you entered her life, Icherra. So, yeah, you have a part in this. If you want your wife back, you're going to tell me everything you know."

Luke scrubbed his face with one hand. Shit. The agent was right. Emily's life did go to hell the minute he stepped back into it. *Emily, I'm so, so sorry*. What he would give to say those words to her. He had nothing to hide. Luke spread his hands. "What is it you want to know?"

"Where is the money your father took from your uncle?"

"What money?" said Luke.

"Don't," growled Webb. "Don't you play stupid with me, Icherra. One and a half million dollars disappeared from the evidence room, not coincidentally when your father, your mother, and you went into witness protection. So, again, where is that money?"

Is he fucking kidding me? Luke thought. This is what the agent was worried about? Money missing two decades back? Fury rose and slung out Luke's next words to Webb.

The very sad thing was that giving up that money would do more to hurt Luke and Emily than keeping it in its hidey hole. This is why Luke didn't mess with it in the first place. But more than that, admitting to having money gained in a criminal enterprise would destroy his chance of staying in the United States. Webb had to know the stakes involved for Luke in admitting he had the money., "My wife's missing and you want me to play twenty questions? If I knew anything about this money about which you are speaking—which I don't—I would give it to you. Shit! I'd have used it long ago. I've got a wife about to have a baby, and we have barely a penny saved! I'd give you anything I had if it meant getting my wife back. Because nothing, and I mean nothing, is more important than her."

Webb didn't even blink in the face of Luke's outburst. "You're real good at playing the victim, Icherra. We both know you're talking a load of shit."

"Not when it comes to my wife, asshole. I mean every word. Now, if you're going to do anything constructive to get my wife back, call me." Luke pushed past Webb as the agent kept his gaze on him.

"Did you ever think, Icherra, that your wife was kidnapped to hold something over your head for you to give up that money?"

Luke turned, spreading his arms and putting his hands on the door jamb. He glared, knowing his eyes looked more Icherra than Wade. "That better not be the story, Webb. Because it seems to me that a very small number of people, myself not included, know about something that happened twenty years ago. And most of those would be government agents."

CHAPTER SEVENTEEN

A Family Meeting

Luke stalked out of the interrogation room so fast that Anglotti had to run to catch up.

"Wait up, Wade," said Anglotti.

"What do you want?" spit Luke. He was thoroughly angry now and past the point to exercise patience with Anglotti. Fuck the police! They weren't ever going to help him. They hadn't in over two decades.

"Hey, Wade. Chill. I didn't call the FBI."

"You didn't need to. Apparently these guys keep me in their sights 24/7. I've got one big target on my back that says, 'Here's the drug lord's nephew. Let's make sure he stays in shit so deep he can never get clear.' This is bullshit!"

Anglotti pushed Luke into an office off the hallway. "This," hissed Anglotti. "This is what I was talking about. You've got to keep your fucking cool, Wade. Yeah, I get that there are bigger things going on. Don't you get it? I live with this shit every fucking day of my life. One eye is on my family and one over my shoulder so that my bosses don't figure out who my family is."

Luke froze, eye to eye with Anglotti. It hit him that Anglotti walked the same tightrope he did, probably even more intensely. While Luke had disowned his criminal family connections, Anglotti had no choice but walk a shadowy line between his and his work. "Okay. Okay. I'll cool down. It's tough. No one seems to be interested in finding Emily."

"Luke, again, you don't get it. The police don't prevent crimes, they don't interrupt crimes; they just file the paperwork afterward."

"I'm sure your bosses don't see it that way."

"You're right. They don't. But I've done this job long enough to know that ninety-five percent of the time that's what it amounts to. Once in a while we'll score a win and the press will make a big deal of it. But so much more gets past us. And those of us who try to do something about the problems of the world have to live with that. But right now what you and I have to do is concentrate on those people who can solve your problem for you. In a while, the FBI team will show up and they'll want to set up a base to work from."

"What can they do?"

"Electronic stuff that I'd have to get a warrant for. Maybe they can get a location from Emily's phone. In the meantime, you need to get to the Red Bull. My uncle wants to talk to you."

"What about the FBI team?"

"Does Tony have the codes to get into your shop?"

Luke must be tired. It took him a moment to connect the name Tony with Saks, which was Saks' real name. "Yeah. Of course."

"Good. I'll send him when they get here. Go. Uncle Vits is waiting for you."

"Isn't Webb going to get all curious about where I'm going?"

"He does seem like the curious type. Don't worry. You need to check on your mother-in-law, don't you? Isn't that what you just told me?"

"Yeah," said Luke. "I suppose I did."

Luke flew down Route 66 and made it the Red Bull in fifteen minutes. Though there were cars in the parking lot, it wasn't the usual mix of motorcycles and SUVs that graced the watering hole each evening. When Luke reached the door, he found the sign that read, 'Closed for regular business for a private party. Thank you for patronizing the Red Bull.' When he pulled on the door, it was locked.

What the hell? He was told to come here. The door was thick, so it wasn't as if he could knock on the thing and people would hear him. He thought he might try the back door, but then the lock turned in the front and pushed open.

Saks stood there. "Come in, Luke. We were waiting on you." His voice carried an urgent tone that Luke wasn't accustomed to hearing from him.

The bar was dark, with only the wall sconces lit. For the first time in Luke's memory, the lights above the bar were turned off. The scent of beer and liquor that clung to walls was highlighted by the lack of illumination.

"In back of the bar," said Saks.

Luke followed Saks to the section behind the bar. Here, a long stretch of tables was set up to end. There weren't as many men here as the night when he was here in similar circumstances. He recognized John and Shelton Rocco, but the others he did not know. This didn't surprise him. But what did surprise him was who was tied to a chair, sitting on the platform in the corner where bands set up.

Pez.

He stepped closer to see the one-percenter sporting a shiner on his right eye.

Alarmed, Luke spun around. "What the hell's going on here?" Was he about to be filled with lead?

"Luke," said Saks quietly, "you need to keep calm. They were trying to help you, and you should show them respect."

"Fuck! Don't you know holding this man will start a gang war?"

"Of course we know," said a gravelly voice.

Luke was absolutely shocked. This was a disaster, an absolute cluster-fuck.

"Luke, meet my Uncle Vito, though we call him Vits for short. He's the capo for our group."

"Capo?"

"Like captain. He and a couple others report directly to the head of our family. In this area, he's the boss." Saks took Luke's arm and spoke low in his ear. "And I mean it about the respect thing."

"Got it," replied Luke.

"Mr. Wade," said Vits, "You've been very good to our Anthony here. He speaks highly of you. Tells us you are an honorable man. We cannot say the same thing about your uncle, Raymond Icherra. He came here offering things and making promises. But we think he had no intention of keeping any of them. Knowing we were here, he was playing us against other elements of this state. You know who we are speaking about."

Luke nodded. It had to be the Rojos and the Hombres. "Yes, sir."

"This man here, Pez, he has some interesting information. But he says he'll not tell us the full story unless you are here. So we asked you to come."

Luke stepped closer to the stage. "Pez?"

"Hah," sneered Pez. "Don't get all excited, *pendajo*. I just didn't want to die without taking you down."

"What a sense of drama," said Vits. "We aren't going to kill you."

"Not yet, anyway," said another man at the table, whose face was shadowed.

There were grim chuckles at the table, but, Luke reflected, this was not helping the situation at hand.

"Pez," said Luke, "if you have something to say, I suspect you'd better spit it out. These men don't play. They have a reputation to uphold."

"Yeah, such honorable men."

Shelton Rocco, the owner of the bar, stepped over to Pez and backhanded him hard in the jaw. Luke stood facing the two, stock-still and not breathing. For as many years as he'd known Rocco, he'd never seen him so much as snap at a customer.

"Pez," said Luke, "I suspect things can get much worse for you, so stop playing hard ball."

"After all we've meant to each other, *pendajo*, you just want me to roll over and play the whore? I'm fucking crushed."

"Vits," sighed Shelton, "I think it's time to take out the trash."

"Okay, okay," said Pez. "It's like this, *pendajo*. There's something crooked going with the G-men. They're looking for something you supposedly have. Someone from there hired a couple of my guys to go looking around your property, but they mucked it up."

Luke remembered the night he'd had to go shut off the security alarm and did the walk-through with the police. "Yeah, and so? Wait. Were these the same guys who kidnapped my wife?"

Pez's face turned red. "These guys hire out for anything or anyone. I didn't know anything about it."

"But you know these guys. Where did they take my wife?"

"I don't know anything about that, and those *cabrons* disappeared, so I can't ask them."

"Asshole!" exploded Luke. He wanted to tear the man apart, but Saks was holding on to his arms, tight.

"Let's save this for the jerks when we find them, Luke."

Vits spoke up. "Now, *pendajo*, is that the term you use? Interesting word. Can mean so many things, but in this case I think it means 'I'm-going-spill-my-guts-if-I-know-what's-good-for-me.' So, *pendajo*, what's going on with Ray Icherra?"

Pez glared at Vits. "Nothing," he spat.

"Shelton," said Vits wearily.

The owner of the bar stepped in closer to Pez and raised his fist.

"Mother of—Oh, *puto culo,* okay, enough! Enough. The bastard wanted to supply us with enough *leillo* to put you out of business."

"Cocaine," hissed Vits.

"*Si.*"

"And he did this to some Hombres leadership and then the Rojos."

"Si, the *cabron* did that. "

"He offered us the same thing," said Vits.

Pez offered a crooked smile. "Guess he didn't know we were already business partners."

Vits frowned. "But you violated one term of our agreement."

"Which is?"

"Don't get the local cops excited. And that is what you did when you allowed your men to kidnap Wade's wife. You know they've been watching Luke because of his connection with Icherra."

"I didn't—" started Pez

"Are you telling me that you don't have control over your crew? Because that makes you look weak. What would you rather be? Weak or stupid?"

Pez started swearing a long streak in Spanish.

"Take him to the van. We have another visitor."

Pez twisted and spit as two men Luke didn't know untied and pulled Pez out of the chair. He struggled, but the two men were larger than him. They dragged him out the back door.

"*Stupido,*" said Vits. "I told him I wasn't going to kill him."

The other men, also shadowed, laughed like it was a joke.

"What're you going to do to him?" asked Luke.

"What does it matter?" said Vits.

"I'd like the opportunity to pound the crap out of him." He shrugged. "After I get my wife back, of course."

"You might get to do that, but not here. Not now. This is a place for business, not personal vendettas. Shelton, John. Our next guest."

"I'll never get over it," muttered Vits. "Shelton. What the fuck kind of name is that?"

"My wife's father," snapped another man who Luke couldn't see. "Now shut up about it."

If Luke thought that the wise guys hauling Pez out was bad, the next person they brought in was worse.

John and Shelton brought in Raymondo Icherra, his hands bound before him. His eyes bounced around the scene, taking in the men at the table, and then Luke and Saks. He held his head up when he saw Luke.

"Mr. Icherra," said Vits, "or should I say *Senor* Icherra, I'm giving you one chance, and one chance only, to come clean about the purpose of your visit here."

"Why would I?" snarled Icherra. His eyes, darting around the room, sizing up the men there, were dangerous and feral enough to elicit a shiver from Luke. *Here*, thought Luke, *is where I came from*. The thought turned his stomach.

"Because," spit Vits, "you've stirred up a lot of trouble in your short time here. Some of the spic factions are ready to go at each other because of your little offers, and I'm telling your right now, we settled one spic war this past summer. If not for how that stirs up the cops, we wouldn't bother."

"Don't talk so big," said Icherra, his tone a nasty slur. "You were ready to deal with me."

"No. We were ready to listen to you. We got an earful and we didn't like what you said. And I think that's how you wanted it. You wanted to cause trouble, hoping that it would draw law enforcement's attention away from what you really wanted to accomplish: to get your nephew and his wife out of the country."

Icherra scoffed. "Why would I do that?"

"Because it makes it harder for Luke to get citizenship based on his kid's birth here, which is a change the president is trying to put into law. And he'll probably do it."

"You fucking asshole!" Luke was beside himself. "Where is Emily, you bastard?"

Icherra blinked. "What're you talking about?"

"Emily was kidnapped from our apartment today!"

"What? You think I did that?"

"That was your plan, wasn't it?"

"You together, if I could convince you. I thought having the cops in your business might do that. But no, Ray. I would not take your bride. I wanted you to come willingly with me, home to Mexico. You're all the family I have left."

"Why should I believe what you say? Why would you care about family? You killed my parents, you fucking piece of shit."

"Is that what that bastard told you?"

"What bastard? There are so many in my life."

"Agent Reginald Harkness. Isn't that a pussy name? Reginald?" He grinned at the wise guys and a few chuckled back. Icherra turned his head back to Luke.

"I swear on my mother's grave, your grandmother, Ray, I didn't kill my brother or your mother. I let him run, let him take the money, because I cared about what happened to all three of you. If my brother could make a better life in America, so be it. I cannot help it if that *sarambiche* Harkness got him all paranoid about what I could do to him."

Luke closed his eyes, remembering with sadness and anger the day Reggie told him about his parents dying, and later, about who'd killed them. *What a damned liar*, Luke thought. Rage filled him, an absolute anger toward the man.

The man who'd killed his parents.

"Do you know where he is?" demanded Luke. He stared first at Icherra, who shook his head, and then at the wise guys, all of whom gazed at Luke impassively.

"Not yet," said Vits. "But we're looking."

The words Pepper spoke to him, that seemed like ages ago, crossed his mind. *This is part of a broader investigation.*

"I might know someone who can help us with that."

CHAPTER EIGHTEEN

Trickster

While the Roccos escorted Icherra to the back room in the bar, Luke dialed a number on his phone he hadn't used in a while. "Pepper."

"Yeah."

"Come to the Red Bull."

"What the hell, Luke. Why?"

"Because I have information about that broader investigation you were talking about."

"Then tell me."

"No. In person. Now." Luke hung up the phone and looked toward the men whose faces he didn't see.

"I just invited a DEA agent here. At least I think he's DEA. I don't know. I also don't know if someone is bugging his phone."

"Gentlemen," said Vits. "I believe our general business here is concluded."

There were murmurs of agreement around the table, and one by one they pushed away, spoke a few quiet words to Vits, and headed out the back door. Only Vits, John, and Shelton, who came back into the main bar, remained.

John and Shelton moved through the room, putting on the lights, and separating tables. Luke helped with the last part and mating chairs with tables. Finally, after the bar looked open, John unlocked the door and pulled in the sign as Vits moved to the darkest corner of the Red Bull with a beer in hand.

John walked to bar and tossed the sign under. "Luke," the bartender said as he pulled a draft from the tap, "have a seat."

Luke took the offered beer and sat at a table that faced the door. He was resolved to get some answers and soon retrieve his wife.

Ninety-five percent of the time all we do is file the paperwork, Anglotti told him. No way was Luke going to let Emily become paperwork.

Finally, after what felt like forever, the door pushed open and Pepper strolled in.

"Your usual?" said John.

"Yes. Quiet here tonight," replied Pepper.

John shrugged. "That might not last long." He laid out a shot of Jose Cuervo and a Corona on the bar. Pepper tried to pay him, but John nodded toward Luke. "It's on Luke."

Luke waved Pepper to sit with him at the table.

Pepper settled at the table opposite Luke and took a long pull of his Corona, keeping his eyes on him.

"So," said Pepper finally. "What was that phone call about?"

"I want to know where Reggie Harkness is."

"Who's that?"

"You know damn well who that is. He's the guy who put my parents and me into witness protection and then killed them three years later."

The DEA agent sighed. "I can't help you, Luke." He stood and then faced Shelton Rocco, who had moved quietly from the kitchen when Pepper sat. Since Rocco had six inches on him, Pepper was forced to look up to see his face. Pepper turned back to Luke.

His eyes narrowed and his muscles tightened as he put his hands on the table. "What's this about, Luke?"

"What this is about, Hector, is murder and kidnapping."

"Kidnapping," he said slowly.

"Yes. Emily was kidnapped from our home today, Hector. She's supposed to avoid stress and requires medication."

"I, I," he stuttered. "Oh, shit."

"Oh shit, indeed. How is it that you didn't know about this?"

"Because," said a deeper voice at the door. "I didn't tell him."

Both John and Shelton stared shocked at the incarnation of Gibs, who entered the Red Bull.

"Rob," said Hector.

"You know him?" Luke could have been pushed over by a feather.

"What did I tell you about staying away from Wade, huh?"

"Look, you fucker," growled Luke. "You'd better tell me what the hell's going on! What do you know about this? Where's Emily?"

"As far as we can tell, Emily is fine. We're waiting on Harkness, to make a move to take him in. Otherwise, we're afraid it's going to devolve into a firefight."

"Just exactly who," said Shelton, "is we?"

"FBI," said Hector.

"See, this is exactly the problem," said Rob in a disapproving tone. "You can't help but tell him everything, can you?"

"Luke's good people," said Pepper, "and has been in the middle of this intra-agency shit for far too long. Look, Luke, your father stole a good amount of money from his brother. When your father was brought in, Harkness confiscated the money. Then the money went missing. We think Harkness stole it but your father stole it from him. He's been looking for that money ever since."

"He won't find it," said a gravelly voice from behind the bar area. Icherra stepped into the light. He looked at the Roccos. "Boys, there isn't a lock that can hold me." From his dark corner, Vits chuckled.

"Who's that?" said Rob, alarmed. He reached inside his jacket.

"Whoa. Just my uncle," said Luke. "No one you need to worry about if we get a straight story from you."

"Regardless," said Icherra. "My brother didn't steal nothing from me. I gave him that money, with my blessing. I did this so he could buy a new life in America with his wife, a lovely woman, by the way, and my nephew."

"Still money gained in a criminal enterprise," glowered Rob.

"Prove it," challenged Icherra. When Rob didn't say anything, Icherra said, "Yeah, that's just the problem. There was no proof. Just a whole bunch of shit spit out by corrupt federals looking to score easy money off some people afraid of them. Ray, don't believe for a second your parents entered the country illegally. I helped them get the visas myself. There are records in Mexico. The rest," he glared then at Pepper, "is on Harkness and the agency he worked for."

"Ray, I hope someday you'll forgive me for not telling you. I really did hope you'd come home to Mexico with me and get out of this snake's nest of a country."

"I like my country just fine," said Luke. "It's just some people I'm not fond of."

"Yeah. I can see why."

"Shit, Luke. I'm sorry," said Pepper. "Obviously I was kept in the dark."

"Save it for your review board," snarled Rob. "You blew it when you got Wade kicked out of his club."

"You weren't doing anything to protect him."

"That is where you were wrong, Gonzales. I was watching them the whole time."

"Wait, you got me kicked out to protect me?"

"Okie played along because it looked like, with the shit your uncle kicked up, the Rojos and Hombres were going to come after the Spawn. He let it be known the Spawn were more than happy to buy his cocaine if they didn't."

"So I laid it on a little thick," said Icherra. "And damn, looks like it worked. We're all talking now and getting straight answers."

"Damned trickster," muttered Rob.

Icherra just smiled.

Rob pulled out a phone from his pocket. "Gibson. Yeah. Okay. I'll be there in a few. Okay, Wade. You're up. The team got a call that Harkness wants to talk to you. Don't worry. Your man Saks answered the phone. Harkness doesn't know we're on the job."

"Just like that I'm supposed to go with you?"

"You're right. It would look out of character if you showed up alone. Gonzales, call Oakland Walker and get him and some of the Spawn out to that donut shop on Route 5 between Route 9 and Interstate 691. They'll be good window-dressing for when Luke walks across the street to meet with Harkness at the hotel."

Luke twisted his wedding ring on his finger. Most times he didn't pay attention to the ring. But on this day, with his worry for his wife shot sky high, his hand went to the one thing that was a tangible reminder of the woman he loved.

He stood inside the 24-hour donut shop, looking out the window across the lighted highway to the large hotel that loomed lit with floods against the dark of the night. Emily was there, among strangers, probably afraid. The frustration of not being able to go to her now ate him up from the inside. But the FBI agent with him told him he had to wait.

"We've got to make it look good. They have people watching. Even though they told you to come alone, Harkness isn't stupid enough to think you would."

The bulletproof vest Rob insisted he wore felt bulky under his clothing. *Hang on, Em*, he thought. *I'll be there soon.*

Rob brought over two coffees and placed them on the table next to Luke. Pepper was posted outside in Rob's SUV, keeping an eye on movement around the hotel with night binoculars.

"What's your story, Gibson?" asked Luke, still staring out the window.

"What story is that?"

"Why did you run out on Amanda when she told you she was pregnant?"

Gibson's face drained of color. "You know about that?"

"When you showed up at my apartment when Amanda was there, you blew your own cover."

"Yeah. I didn't expect her to be there." Rob twisted his cup. "I admit it. I was young. And stupid, and unfortunately, before I knew about the kid, I had enlisted in the army. I couldn't afford college and I thought that was the best thing to do. I didn't have a job or an education to get a good one. Things were quiet then in the spring and I thought I could do stateside duty. Amanda was going to college and I thought we could visit during school breaks and things. When I got out, I could go to school on the GI Bill. It would be a slow road but we'd get there, marriage, a house, a family."

"So you wanted to marry her."

"Sure, but her family hated me, and I didn't measure up."

"I know that story."

"I thought if I made something of myself..." He drew a deep breath. "But I messed that up. I didn't tell her I enlisted. Chicken shit, actually. I knew she'd be upset. So I avoided her. Second worst mistake I ever made, besides leaving. But I signed those papers and Uncle Sam owned me, so I had to go. I was late actually reporting, and when I got home after the prom the MPs were waiting at the house." He sighed, partially lost in old memories. "Later, I found out she married Sam Dougherty. I called her once, on her birthday, to wish her well. I heard my baby, Emily, crying in the background, and then Dougherty hung up on me. I deserved it for being such a coward."

"That's it?" Luke couldn't imagine leaving the woman he loved or his kid.

"I won't tell you the rest of it, because I took stupid chances with my life. But the Army called me a hero and pinned metals on me. Ironic, really... Pinned for courage when I couldn't face my own life. After I got out, I applied to the FBI and have been there ever since. And when the file hit my desk about a MC club in my hometown mixed up with the Mafia, I took it. I didn't know Emily was involved."

"Wait. Who filed that case with the FBI?"

"Hector Gonzales, the guy you call Pepper."

"You know the Spawn wasn't involved with the Mafia?"

"Yeah," he said with a crooked smile, "but it was the only way Hector could get traction with this so the FBI would investigate Moyes and Harkness, so he played that angle. And you can't exactly say, after tonight, you aren't mixed up with the Mafia. They've got your back, for what reason I don't know, but they do."

Luke nodded, connecting the dots.

Rob continued, "And Hector, he seemed like a good guy on the DEA side of things, so I requested he work with me. But he kept running to you trying to get you to back off, so I had to keep him out of the loop." He slugged his coffee like it was a shot of alcohol. "And that, Raymondo Icherra, aka Luke Wade, is the story."

CHAPTER NINETEEN

Rescue

Okie and several of the Spawn in club jackets entered the donut shop. Spider broke off and went to the counter to order coffees.

"Luke," said Okie, tightly studying Luke's reaction.

"Okie," said Luke. He sat at the table and studied his coffee, which was still filled to the brim.

"And you," said Okie coldly, speaking to Rob. "Gibs was right. You could have been twins. Didn't know you were a G-man."

"No one in the family knew. I worked undercover many years. I told them I was in jail so they wouldn't come looking for me."

"I see. You gave Helen a lotta shit."

"Yeah. I'm sorry about that. I had to make it seem like I was in town for a reason. I'll make it up to her somehow."

"Where's Pepper?"

"I have him watching the movements at the hotel."

"And Saks?"

"At my shop," said Luke. "Babysitting the crack team to help recover Emily."

"Luke, you have to know, I was only looking out for your interests. I only wanted you to stay away, out of the line of fire."

"Nice of you to care. But if you've noticed, I'm a big boy."

"Sure. I can admit when I'm wrong. You're part of Hades' Spawn and always will be if you want it. That goes for Saks too. I can't fault a man for loyalty."

Luke nodded. It was good to know he was welcomed back, but he wasn't sure how far he could trust Okie after what happened. "We'll talk about it later. I have an appointment with my wife's kidnappers."

"What do you want us to do?"

"Just stand outside the shop here," said Rob, "and do what you do best: look menacing. If you want to play-act, make it look like you want to go with Luke, but he pushes you off. But if people start shooting, hit the pavement."

"Thanks for the heads-up," grumbled Okie.

The other Spawn muttered similar sentiments.

"Knock it off, you guys," said Okie. "We're here to help Luke, not get in a pissing match."

Rob put his phone to his ear.

"Yeah. Right. Is everyone in position? Good."

Rob put his hand on Luke's shoulder. "You're up, son."

With a final look at the men who had been his brothers, and the man who was less than a father to Emily than the man who raised her, Luke walked out of the donut shop.

The Spawn followed Luke and did as Rob suggested. Okie pretended he was going to walk with him, and Luke made a show of pushing him off. Setting his jaw, he walked across the four-lane highway, watching for traffic. But it was late, and the traffic quiet. He made it across without incident.

Luke felt as if eyes were watching him. He wasn't sure if it was Rob's assault team or Harkness' people, or even both. He kept his head up and his shoulders back. He wasn't going to show fear. Emily's life could depend on the performance he gave here.

The face that Luke had grown to hate when he was a child stepped out from the hotel lobby. The FBI team, through Saks, told him the only way Luke would meet him was out in the open.

Reginald Harkness still had that thin-beaked nose and thin lips that Luke learned to associate with cruelty. His dark hair was now salt and pepper.

"Ray," said Reggie, as he slung his arm across Luke's back.

"Get your hands off me, you bastard," growled Luke.

"Sure," said Reggie icily, "as long as you have something for me."

"Yeah," said Luke. "Here's the bank's name, the account number, and the password."

"A Bahama bank account? Nice. Sounds like a good place for a vacation."

"Yeah, asshole. Now, where's my wife?"

"Not so fast. I have to verify the money is there. Mi Reyito? That's the password?"

"Yeah. My uncle's nickname for me."

Reggie grunted and pulled up the online banking information. He stood, concentrating on the screen for several minutes, while Luke felt like pounding the man's face into the pavement. But any misfire at this point could spoil everything, so Luke waited. "Got it. Transfer in place. Clear out, guys," he said into a mic at his shoulder. "We're good to go. Thanks for the cash, kid. Though it took me long enough to get it. Seems a little short. Two million? What happened to the interest?"

Luke flashed a smile. This is what he was waiting for.

"I had expenses."

Reggie looked up from his phone, puzzled, and then realization dawned as two SUVs swung in and six agents in black body armor and rifles jumped out and surrounded them. Reggie made a desperate grab for Luke, but Luke saw the movement and jumped back to avoid him. He watched with satisfaction as one agent shoved Reggie to the ground and another zip-tied his hands behind his back. He bent next to Reggie.

"Thing is, Reggie, the money isn't in the Bahamas, and you'll be tied up a long time, so you won't be vacationing there either. Where the fuck's my wife?"

Rob, out of breath from running across the highway, stood over Reggie. "Gotcha. Took me a while, but I got you. And your buddy, Moyes, he's in custody too. And Luke, she's in room 326. We have an ambulance on the way."

Luke, heart pounding in his chest, ran into the hotel, and, not willing to wait for the elevator, found the stairs and raced up them. At the third floor, he flung open the door and ran toward the door where a body- armored agent stood and tried to hold him back. "That's my wife in there." He pushed past the guard and tore into the room.

Emily lay on the bed, still and unmoving. Luke's heart pushed up into his throat. "Emily!" He crossed to the bed, looking desperately for the rise and fall of her chest. "Baby?" His heart stopped as he looked at his wife. Her face had lost its rosy color. "Oh fuck. No!" he groaned.

Emily stirred, her eyes fluttered open. "Luke?" She swallowed and tried to lick her lips, and gave him a half smile. "I knew you'd find me."

And his heart started again.

CHAPTER TWENTY

New Folder

The warm sun beat down on Luke and he sighed. The blue waters of the Caribbean lapped the sand and a light breeze played over his skin. This was what he'd needed, what they'd both needed. He glanced over at Emily, who shaded her eyes with one hand while she looked at her phone.

"Put it away, Em," Luke said. "Little Robbie's fine."

"I don't know why I let you talk me into this," fussed Emily. "He's too young for extended overnights."

"He's thirteen months, Em. He can walk and everything. I even saw him drinking from the sippy cup on his own."

"See how much we're missing?"

In one swift move, Luke swung off his lounger to straddle Emily's legs. His eyes ran over Emily's oiled body with appreciation. The swell of her breasts in her swimsuit was especially appealing since she kept more of them after her pregnancy than she had before. He licked his lips. "You know what I miss? Some alone time with my wife."

"Hey, we get date nights."

"Uh-huh, with you itching to get back to collect Robbie from your sister or your mother. Call me greedy, but I want more." He put his hands on either side of her breasts and cupped them in his hand.

"We're out in public here," said Emily.

"Which is why I rented the cabana." He leaned over and crushed his mouth to her lips. Her mouth opened and their tongues tangled, colliding with rising frenzy. Emily's breathing hitched as Luke pressed his growing shaft between her legs. "You're beautiful, Mrs. Wade," he whispered.

"You'll have to watch out for my husband," she said coyly. "He doesn't like it when I pick up beach bums."

"Beach bum, eh? Does he like it when you pick up anyone?"

"Oh no. He's a very possessive man."

"What would happen if he caught you?"

"I'm afraid I'd be punished with hours of him eating me out, and then," she sighed dramatically, "hours and hours of lovemaking. It's really quite awful."

"I can see where you're abused. Here, let me make you forget your terrible husband." He stood and hauled her up, pressing her body against his. He nuzzled her neck with soft kisses and nips on her neck. Emily moaned.

He cupped her gorgeous ass in his hands. This was another area that got meatier during her pregnancy and didn't change "AB," after baby. However, he didn't dare tell her that. But he loved how the cheeks of her derrière filled out her jeans more fully. It just made him want to dive in between them and do wicked things, especially when he walked behind her. He gave them a hard squeeze, which made Emily squeal.

Luke couldn't believe that he'd love Emily any more than when he married her, but every day with her he seemed to love her more. Watching her give birth to their son branded him with an appreciation of just how extraordinary she was. That was probably the happiest day of his life. And seeing how she cared for Robbie warmed his heart every day. It made him want to be the best father he could be.

The second happiest day was when the immigration judge cleared the way for Luke's permanent citizenship. Citing "the egregious actions of a corrupt government official that prevented the natural course of events in obtaining citizenship," the judge ordered that Luke be allowed to apply for citizenship without any impediments from the immigration department. A month later, Luke took the oath that finally made him a citizen of the United States.

Perhaps the third happiest day was when Emily reconciled with Sam. When she was released from the hospital that day she was rescued, Sam was there and thanked Luke for bringing his baby girl home. Immediately, and without hesitation, she hugged him and called him Dad. From that point on, Sam Dougherty accepted Luke as his own son, just as he did Justin. However, if Sam ever found out what Luke engineered for Justin's bachelor party, that attitude might change.

Another happy day was seeing Reggie arraigned for murder, kidnapping, extortion, and a dozen related charges. He couldn't make bail, proving that crime does not pay, and was awaiting trial. Rob had built a compelling case for the murder of Luke's parents, of which Luke was glad. He'd like nothing more than to see that asshole locked up for the rest of his life.

Rob came by before he left town and introduced himself to Emily. She was cordial and gracious but didn't open up to him as a daughter. They sent letters to each other, but often Rob was on the road or undercover for a case, so there were long stretches when they don't communicate. Emily didn't mind one way or the other.

Things weren't so copasetic with Hades' Spawn. Okie disappointed Luke with how he treated him, despite his good intentions. Luke wasn't sure if he could ever forgive him. He took back his patch but resigned his office of vice president, which went to Spider. Luke attended some club functions, which were held in his clubhouse for the Spawn, but mainly he kept up his association with the Spawn for the health of his business.

"Baby," said Emily. "Hey, it seemed like I lost you there for a minute."

Luke smiled. "I got lost in your luscious curves." He put his head between her breasts and licked the cleft between them. "Mmm, delicious."

"You're incorrigible."

"Did you say I'm encouragable?"

"That too."

Luke took her hand and pulled her along to the cabana, their feet dancing on the hot sand. Sweeping her off her feet, he pushed aside the canvas and set her down on the extra wide chaise. Gripping her bikini bottom, he pulled it off, with Emily squealing in surprise.

"Why, sir, I do believe you have dishonorable intentions."

He plopped down between her splayed legs. "And that's just the beginning. I plan on getting you good and ready." His mouth met her mound, and he worked his tongue all around, licking her cleft and the soft folds on either side of her clit. She moaned, lightly at first and then more urgently. Emily got wetter and not just from his tongue. Luke tasted her sweet juices, and this just got him hotter. He couldn't wait to get inside her, to feel her hot, velvety flesh surrounding his. He speared her with his tongue, exploring and teasing.

She whimpered, and it drove him on. He laid his tongue on her clit once again, and this time lashed it mercilessly as she writhed under him. Emily pulled his head into her mound and ground against his lips and tongue.

"Baby, I'm cumming," she gasped.

She bucked against his face and moaned. It was such a sweet sound Luke didn't mind holding his breath until he could breathe again. This was something else he loved about his wife, how she gave herself to him and the experience totally.

Finally, she calmed, and with a wicked smile Luke rose up and captured her lips, sharing her nectar on his lips with his sweet, sweet wife.

"Oh, sweet lord, that was amazing," she said.

"That was just a warm-up." He grinned wickedly at her.

She lifted her eyebrows. "You're a sinful man."

Luke gave her a lazy wink. He pulled off her bikini top, revealing the round globes of her breasts, and couldn't resist pinching them with his fingers.

"Oh," said Emily.

He descended on her breasts, sucking one pink nipple, then another in sharply, and twirling his tongue over the sensitive bud of her nipple.

Emily arched her back each time, whimpering, "I don't, no, oh, oh, fuck, more, please."

He loved to hear her babble like that as she edged closer to losing control. Breathing in her sexy musk, tasting her salty skin, Luke was close to losing it himself. His cock was hard and ready, throbbing, demanding it get its prize.

"Baby, I'm going to make you feel so good," he breathed. "I've been waiting for this." His hand found her sensitive clit and rubbed it lightly. But it was her core he wanted, and he slid two fingers into her. Moisture and heat surrounded them and he easily imagined his cock inside her.

Emily's hips rose and fell against his finger, and her head thrashed on the pillow. She wasn't there, not yet, but close, and Luke was rapidly losing the will to hold back. There was only one thought in his mind now.

"Baby," he breathed. "Are you ready?" He knew the answer. Luke just liked asking the question.

Emily whimpered some more, a sound of desperation now.

Yes. Now.

With a shake of his hips and pulling with his hands, he got free of his swimsuit. He took his cock in hand and gave himself two good strokes. His cock leaked pre-cum. Swiping his fingers across the head, he gathered that elixir on his fingers. Luke held his fingers to Emily's mouth. "Suck on this, baby."

As she opened her mouth to take his fingers, he guided his cock between her legs and entered, holding the head just inside her entrance. Her juices flowed around him, calling him to fill her.

She gasped, and he smiled.

"Yeah, sweetheart. You're good and ready. And I think it's time for another baby."

Emily's orgasm broke upon them with a rush as Luke finally slid home.

The End

Hades' Spawn Motorcycle Club Series

One You Can't Forget
Book 1
One That Got Away
Book 2
One That Came Back
Book 3
One You Never Leave
Book 4

Note from Lexy Timms:

I hope you enjoyed the Hades' Spawn series as much as I enjoyed writing it! I feel blessed every day that I get to do to what I love. Thank you for letting me write, and dream, and imagine... oh and have a new book-boyfriend ever other week, lol!

I love hearing from readers so catch me on one of these links!

Lexy

xx

Lexy Timms Newsletter:

http://eepurl.com/9i0vD

Lexy Timms Facebook Page:

https://www.facebook.com/SavingForever

Lexy Timms Website:

http://lexytimms.wix.com/savingforever

NEW
One Christmas Night
Hades' Spawn Christmas Novella
Now Available!

Luke and Emily have each other, and their toddler son, but every other relationship in their lives is strained—the result of the violent events revolving around the Spawn and the club's president two years before.

When the president of Hades' Spawn, Oakie Walker, insists Luke and Emily host the club's Christmas Party, Luke's not very happy. Though he was reinstated as a member of the Spawn, and maintains their clubhouse, he spends only the time he has to with the club.

Emily's adoptive father, Sam Dougherty, makes no bones that biker Luke is not good enough for his daughter, while her biological father, Rob, wants to get closer to her and his grandson and no one but Emily is happy about it. Add to the mix that the president of a rival motorcycle club, the Rojos, does everything he can to create the impression that Luke will join his gang, and you have a recipe for one explosive Christmas party.

Can Luke and Emily negotiate the tricky currents of the demands from those around them? Or will it damage their relationship if they do?

NEW SERIES Coming January 2017!

EXCERPT INCLUDED!

Making Her His

Saks' Story

Anthony Parks, AKA Saks straddles two worlds and neither one is very reputable. One is as a motorcycle mechanic and Road Captain of the Hades Spawn, a none too squeaky clean motorcycle club. The other is as the scion of an organized crime family who wants him to join the family business, something he is loathed to do.

Recent events with the Spawn has soured his community reputation, and while certain women like bad boys, those kind of women are not who Saks is looking for. Add pressure from his family that "it is time to marry" Saks is faced with an impossible situation.

His wise-guy uncle proposes an arranged marriage between Saks and the daughter of a dom from another crime family. And when he meets a mysterious blonde that shows him love at first sight is possible, he knows that he could never accept his uncle proposal. Now he would just have to figure out a way to tell Uncle Vits without getting excommunicated from the family or putting the Spawn in the crosshairs of a powerful crime organization. While he is doing that he has to find the woman who has stolen his heart.

Christina

Christina Marie Serafini decided a long time ago that her loving but paternalistic family wasn't going to determine the course of her life. She had no desire to get mixed up in any of the many legal and illegal businesses her family owned. Chrissy had earned a Masters in Business and Communications on her own dime, and she just landed her dream job of Director of Marketing for an up and coming business.

Marriage and a family isn't in her game plan right now and when she did marry it was going to be a respectable man. When her grandfather announced he had arranged a marriage for her with "a nice Italian man," Christina goes ballistic. She wasn't going to marry anyone, let alone someone chosen for her. She certainly wouldn't marry a member from another crime family. Chrissy could only imagine what kind of opportunistic carogna would agree to marry a woman he never met.

Urged by her sister to at least check him out, she goes to his family's bar to confirm her suspicions. That's when she finds a handsome biker that knows exactly how to send her emotions and body into overdrive. But realizing the hunky man is the one her grandfather wants to marry sends her into flight mode even though he haunts her dreams.

Once he finds her can Saks convince the woman of his dreams to look past his family connections to take a chance on a lowly motorcycle mechanic? And if he does, can he look past hers?

COMING January 2017

Making Her His - CHAPTER 1

Saks' Sunday Dinner

"Don't you have a place to be?" His cousin, John Rocco, bartender of the Red Bull, slid a beer toward Saks with his eyebrows arched.

Saks sat at the bar of the Red Bull, which was a second home to him. Even the new clubhouse of the Hades Spawn didn't hold the memories of the Red Bull. He flicked his eyes up to the rafters of the bar where brightly colored bras hung, evidence of the watering hole's rambunctious reputation.

"Yeah. Sunday dinner."

"So?" said John.

Saks shrugged. "So?"

"Aren't you going to be late?"

"In case you haven't noticed, dinner is served twenty-four-seven at my mom's house."

John gave him a "you're-not-getting-the-point" glance and turned to another customer.

Of course, Saks got the point. It was about respect. Uncle Vits, the head of the Rocco family, was going to be there. One did not disrespect the man by showing up late.

But there was something about this day that put Sakes on guard. Part of it was the way his mother insisted that he show up rather than "hang around with that gang of yours." Another was how John made a big deal about Saks being here instead of his parent's house. He didn't know what was going on.

It's not that he didn't love his family. But the fact was he was more than wary of the organized crime aspect of it. He wasn't drawn to their activities, like so many of his other cousins, and he didn't want to make his life around it either. He'd seen too many of his uncles or cousins incarcerated for family crimes taking their jail time as a badge of honor. He didn't think it was either smart or honorable to be involved in illegal activities. His mother backed him on this against his uncle, or rather granduncle, and made sure that Saks' father didn't drag him into the family business.

As a result, Saks lived as an outsider in his own family. Conversations stopped when he entered the room. He didn't hang out with his cousins.

Which was why the Hades Spawn was so important to him.

Well, that, and riding bikes.

Those two things, plus working for Luke Wade, owner of Central Valley Bike Repair, as a motorcycle mechanic made up his life. Unfortunately, his life didn't include a steady girlfriend, which was why he was sitting here at noon on Sunday in a motorcycle hangout bar, killing time.

"Hello."

A pretty brunette slid onto the stool next to him. Her too tight tee that was cut at the midriff advertised what she was looking for.

"I haven't seen you here before," said the brunette with a flash of extra-white teeth.

Saks almost chuckled. "Then you haven't been here often enough," he said

"Buy a girl a drink?" she said.

She didn't even wait to be offered one. Saks didn't like brazen women like this and he could guess what was going to happen next. And it did. She slid her hand on thigh inching her way to his inner leg.

"Which bike out there is yours?" she purred. "I'd love to have a ride."

Of course she would. And she wasn't thinking about riding his bike either.

"John, give the lady here what she wants-on me," said Saks. He then twisted away on the stool.

"You're leaving?" she said in bewilderment.

"I have a family thing. Sorry. Another time." Like no time ever. When he was younger and more impulsive, he would have taken the woman to bed in a heartbeat. But now he was growing older bedding anonymous women lost its shine. At Luke and Emily's wedding that he got an inkling he wanted what they had. Seeing the looks of utter love they gave each other, and watching over these past two years how they stood together against every challenge, he came to realize what he wanted that. Lover. Partner. Best friend.

That would not be this woman, who could be had for the price of a beer and a motorcycle ride.

"See you around," said the woman.

"Sure," said Saks.

Walking away from that woman ease the queasiness in his stomach she elicited. The rumble of his bike's engine shook away the sleazy feeling that clung to him from the woman's touch. Pushing out on the highway eased his mind. His engine sang a song to him, a serenade created from the precision action of pistons perfectly timed to send its life's blood through the engine. Though he drove on blacktop, he felt connected to the earth, wheels on road, sliding seamlessly toward his destination. If it weren't for his roiling thoughts about the family dinner, he would be perfectly at peace.

"Anthony!" said his mother as Saks entered the kitchen door. "Finally you are here. Your Uncle Vits was going crazy thinking you weren't going to show."

Saks kissed his mother on the cheek and took in the familiar Italian restaurant smells of his mother's kitchen. Sauce was bubbling on the stove, and fresh baked Italian bread sat sliced on the table. He reached for a slice but his mother slapped his hand away.

"Of course, I'm here for Sunday dinner. I always am, aren't I? And why is he so anxious today?"

"Here," his mother said as she handed him a platter of fried calamari, "take this to the table."

"Don't you need some help?" he said studying her face. Her bright brown eyes were more lined than usual, and her face seemed drained of color. "You're looking tired, Ma. You should sit down."

"Sush!" she said waving him away. "Terri is helping me."

"Where is my sister?"

"Here I am, Anthony," said Terri. She stood at the top of the basement stair with a long flat tray in her hands. On the tray were freshly made ravioli ready to be cooked.

Saks set down the calamari on the kitchen table.

"Let me help you," he said.

Terri rolled her eyes. "I'm perfectly capable of carrying a tray, thank you very much."

"Sorry," said Saks sarcastically, "for trying to be a gentleman."

Terri stuck her tongue at him while she walked past.

"Take off that jacket," his mother said. Her voice was full of disapproval as she eyed his Hades Spawn leather. "Your uncle will have a fit if he sees it."

Saks shrugged off the cut and hung it carefully on a kitchen chair. "He's good with the club, Mom," he said.

"No," she said. "He tolerates it for your sake." She stared at distaste the club's patch, a skull over a pair of wings. His mothered fingered the leather pulling the front of the jacket closer for her to see. "And what is this? Saks?"

"I've told you before. That's my club name."

"And why do they call you Saks?"

"Because, mom," said Terri setting the ravioli tray on the counter, "Look at him. Khakis? White button down? He dresses better than the rest of them, like Saks of Fifth Avenue? Get it."

His mother rolled her dark eyes again.

"Named after a store. What is wrong with those people?"

"Those people," said Saks, "are my friends." He scooped up a piece of fried calamari and scarfed it down.

"Hey," protested Terri. Saks grinned at her.

"That's for the table," said his mother. "And take it now before it gets cold."

"You need to sit."

"I'll sit after I cook the ravioli."

"I'll do it, ma," said Terri. "Go sit down with dinner. The water boiling is now. It will take five minutes."

Marie Parks grumbled, but she picked up the basket of bread. Saks walked behind her into the dining room where the curtains were drawn tight giving the room a gloomy air. Any other day they would be pulled apart letting the sun in, but today Uncle Vits was visiting.

Uncle Vits sat at the head of the table facing the kitchen while Saks' father stood pouring a glass of wine. The elderly man sat hunched in the chair. He was shorter than most men, a had a rounded belly that led him to play Santa at Christmas for the family. But his sharp, predatory blue eyes commanded the room, giving the distinct impression that anyone that crossed him would feel his wrath.

Vito Rocco was in fact his granduncle, not his uncle which is why Saks' last name was the very Anglo-Saxon name of Parks. Saks' father, Carmello "Whit" Parks, half-Italian from his mother's side, married into the Rocco family by taking Maria Rocco as his wife. His actual grandfather, long since passed was what they euphemistically called "an associate" of Uncle Vits who was "capo" or boss of a good slice of Connecticut. Much of the rest was under the control of their bitter rivals, the Serafini.

"Anthony," said Uncle Vits, "good to see you. Sit. Sit."

Sakes resisted the urge to roll his eyes. It was normal for Vits to act like he was the king in everyone else's house. Saks never understood why other people put up with it, but no one questioned Vito Rocco.

But another thing that was strange about this gathering was that only Vits, not any other member of the extended family sat at the long table. This was more than unusual. It was suspicious. What was going on?

Saks' father poured him a glass of wine as his mother took her place at the head of the table. Terri walked in with the bowl of ravioli. With a spoon she ladled over generous portions to Uncle Vits, her father, her mother and then Saks.

"Hand me that gravy, there, Anthony," said Vits. "And the bread too."

Like many old Italians Vits called tomato sauce gravy. Saks reached over the large salad, the bowl of meatballs, and another of sausage and peppers to grab both items and passed them to his granduncle.

"Grace," reminded his mother. "Anthony, please."

Saks never knew why his mother always chose him to say grace except for maybe she had hoped he would become a priest. Her hope died, however, when Saks refused to go to the seminary college she wanted him to attend. But to get dinner going he made the sign of the cross and the others followed.

"Bless us, oh Lord, and these thy gifts which come from your bounty, through Christ, our Lord. Amen."

"Amen," all at the table affirmed.

Vits laced the ravioli with sauce and took a bite.

"Perfect, Maria, perfect as always. Just like my sainted mother's."

Saks' mother smiled at the compliment.

"Thank you, Uncle Vits."

"And Anthony," said Vits, "how are things for you, eh?"

"Everything's fine," said Saks noncommittally.

"You getting out and having fun?"

"I hang out with my club."

"Yes," hissed Vits. "Your *familia* not good enough for you, eh? But you spend time with that motorcycle club, where Icherra's nephew—"

Vits was referring to Luke, whose uncle, Raymondo Icherra was a Mexican drug lord. But Luke, like Saks, eschewed his criminal family.

"Now, Uncle Vits," chided Terri gently. "This is a nice family gathering, right? Anthony likes his friends."

Vits always had a soft spot for Terri, who he often said was the spitting image of his mother. For this reason she could say things to him that others couldn't.

"Yes, yes," he said waving his hands as if to breeze away his rancorous comments. "A nice family gathering. Sorry." Without a breath he continued the conversation, "So, have you thought about marriage, Anthony?"

"Of course I've thought about it. But I haven't found the right girl."

"So you aren't dating anyone serious?"

"No," said Saks slowly wondering where this intrusive conversation was leading.

"Well, good. There's nice young woman I'd like you to meet. Very pretty. And smart. Very smart. You like that I know."

"Thanks, Uncle Vits, but I can get my own dates."

"No. You don't understand, Anthony. I think she'd make a good wife for you."

Vits spoke with the authority of a Capo, a boss, and Saks looked around at his family's faces. Terri smirked, her mother smiled and his father looked off innocently to the side. But his father, his mother and his sister were no innocents. They were all part of this conspiracy.

"Wife?" said Saks, his voice rising. "Wife? What have you done, Uncle Vits?"

The capo stared at his fingernails.

"Nothing. Not much. Just made a little proposal to the Serafini."

"What!" said Saks jumping to his feet as cold fear rushed through him. "The Serafini? Our rivals?"

"Sit down, Anthony," said Vits dismissively. "It will be good. Good for you. Good for her. Good for business."

Saks sank to his chair under the weight of this mother and father's disapproving glares and knew there was only one thing that was good about this. He was good and fucked.

~ End of Excerpt ~

More by Lexy Timms:

Book One is FREE!

**Sometimes the heart needs a different kind of saving...
find out if Charity Thompson will find a way of saving forever
in this hospital setting Best-Selling Romance by Lexy Timms**

Charity Thompson wants to save the world, one hospital at a time. Instead of finishing med school to become a doctor, she chooses a different path and raises money for hospitals – new wings, equipment, whatever they need. Except there is one hospital she would be happy to never set foot in again—her fathers. So of course he hires her to create a gala for his sixty-fifth birthday. Charity can't say no. Now she is working in the one place she doesn't want to be. Except she's attracted to Dr. Elijah Bennet, the handsome playboy chief.

Will she ever prove to her father that's she's more than a med school dropout? Or will her attraction to Elijah keep her from repairing the one thing she desperately wants to fix?

** This is NOT Erotica. It's Romance and a love story. **

* This is Part 1 of an Eight book Romance Series. It does end on a cliff-hanger*

Managing the Bosses Series
The Boss
Book 1 IS FREE!

Jamie Connors has given up on finding a man. Despite being smart, pretty, and just slightly overweight, she's a magnet for the kind of guys that don't stay around.

Her sister's wedding is at the foreground of the family's attention. Jamie would be find with it if her sister wasn't pressuring her to lose weight so she'll fit in the maid of honor dress, her mother would get off her case and her ex-boyfriend wasn't about to become her brother-in-law.

Determined to step out on her own, she accepts a PA position from billionaire Alex Reid. The job includes an apartment on his property and gets her out of living in her parent's basement.

Jamie has to balance her life and somehow figure out how to manage her billionaire boss, without falling in love with him.

Hades' Spawn MC Series
One You Can't Forget
Book 1 is FREE

Emily Rose Dougherty is a good Catholic girl from mythical Walkerville, CT. She had somehow managed to get herself into a heap trouble with the law, all because an ex-boyfriend has decided to make things difficult.

Luke "Spade" Wade owns a Motorcycle repair shop and is the Road Captian for Hades' Spawn MC. He's shocked when he reads in the paper that his old high school flame has been arrested. She's always been the one he couldn't forget.

Will destiny let them find each other again? Or what happens in the past, best left for the history books?

The Recruiting Trip

Aspiring college athlete Aileen Nessa is finding the recruiting process beyond daunting. Being ranked #10 in the world for the 100m hurdles at the age of eighteen is not a fluke, even though she believes that one race, where everything clinked magically together, might be. American universities don't seem to think so. Letters are pouring in from all over the country.

As she faces the challenge of differentiating between a college's genuine commitment to her or just empty promises from talent-seeking coaches, Aileen heads to the University of Gatica, a Division One school, on a recruiting trip. Her best friend dares who to go just to see the cute guys on the school's brochure.

The university's athletic program boasts one of the top hurdlers in the country. Tyler Jensen is the school's NCAA champion in the hurdles and Jim Thorpe recipient for top defensive back in football. His incredible blue-green eyes, confident smile and rock hard six pack abs mess with Aileen's concentration.

His offer to take her under his wing, should she choose to come to Gatica, is a temping proposition that has her wondering if she might be with an angel or making a deal with the devil himself.

Seeking Justice
Book 1 – is FREE

Rachel Evans has the life most people could only dream of: the promise of an amazing job, good looks, and a life of luxury. The problem is, she hates it. She tries desperately to avoid getting sucked into the family business and hides her wealth and name from her friends. She's seen her brother trapped in that life, and doesn't want it. When her father dies in a plane crash, she reluctantly steps in to become the vice president of her family's company, Syco Pharmaceuticals.

Detective Adrien Deluca and his partner have been called in to look at the crash. While Adrien immediately suspects not everything about the case is what it seems, he has trouble convincing his partner. However, soon into the investigation, they uncover a web of deceit which proves the crash was no accident, and evidence points toward a shadowy group of people. Now the detective needs find the proof.

To what lengths will Deluca go to get it?

Fortune Riders MC Series
NOW AVAILABLE!

Undercover Series - Book 1, PERFECT FOR ME, is FREE!

The city of Pittsburgh keeps its streets safe, partly thanks to Lt. Grady Rivers. The police officer is fiercely intelligent who specializes in undercover operations. It is this set of skills that are sought by New York's finest. Grady is thrown from his hometown onto the New York City underworld in order to stop one of the largest drug rings in the northeast. The NYPD task him with uncovering the identity of the organization's mysterious leader, Dean. It will take all of his cunning to stop this deadly drug lord.

Danger lurks around every corner and comes in many shapes. While undercover, he meets a beauty named Lara. An equally intelligent woman and twice as fearless, she works for a local drug dealer who has ties to the organization. Their sorted pasts have these two become close, and soon they develop feelings for one another. But this is not a "Romeo and Juliet" love story, as the star-crossed lovers fight to survive the deadly streets. Grady treads the thin line between the love he feels for her, and his duties as an officer.

Will he get in too deep?

Heart of the Battle Series
Celtic Viking
Book 1 is FREE!!
In a world plagued with darkness, she would be his salvation.

No one gave Erik a choice as to whether he would fight or not. Duty to the crown belonged to him, his father's legacy remaining beyond the grave.

Taken by the beauty of the countryside surrounding her, Linzi would do anything to protect her father's land. Britain is under attack and Scotland is next. At a time she should be focused on suitors, the men of her country have gone to war and she's left to stand alone.

Love will become available, but will passion at the touch of the enemy unravel her strong hold first?

Fall in love with this Historical Celtic Viking Romance.

* There are 3 books in this series. Book 1 will end on a cliff hanger.

*Note: this is NOT erotica. It is a romance and a love story.

Knox Township, August 1863.

Little Love Affair, Book 1 in the Southern Romance series, by bestselling author Lexy Timms

Sentiments are running high following the battle of Gettysburg, and although the draft has not yet come to Knox, "Bloody Knox" will claim lives the next year as citizens attempt to avoid the Union draft. Clara's brother Solomon is missing, and Clara has been left to manage the family's farm, caring for her mother and her younger sister, Cecelia.

Meanwhile, wounded at the battle of Monterey Pass but still able to escape Union forces, Jasper and his friend Horace are lost and starving. Jasper wants to find his way back to the Confederacy, but feels honor-bound to bring Horace back to his family, though the man seems reluctant.

NOTE: This is romance series, book 1 of 3. All your questions will not be answered in the first book.

Coming Soon:

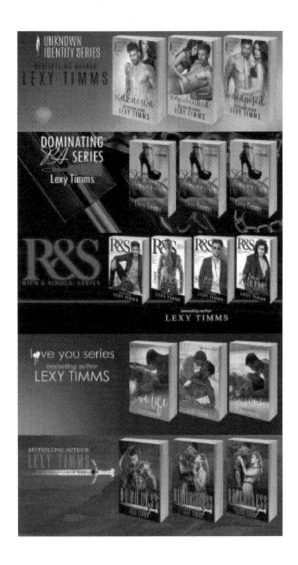

Don't miss out!

Click the button below and you can sign up to receive emails whenever Lexy Timms publishes a new book. There's no charge and no obligation.

Sign Me Up!

https://books2read.com/r/B-A-NNL-WPMI

BOOKS 2 READ

Connecting independent readers to independent writers.

Did you love *One You Never Leave*? Then you should read *Billionaire Biker* by Lexy Timms!

"I look at you and I see the rest of my life in your eyes. I'll love you. Forever."

Katie's not the usual rich girl and Morgan's not your typical biker. The two collide at a bar, and then bump into each after Morgan leaves the scene of a terrible crime.

Falling for one another is inevitable, but when the truth of who Katie is comes out, will it change everything?

Fortune Riders MC Series:

Book 1 - Billionaire Biker

Book 2 - Billionaire Ransom

Book 3 - Billionaire Misery

Also by Lexy Timms

Alpha Bad Boy Motorcycle Club Triology
Alpha Biker

Conquering Warrior Series
Ruthless

Diamond in the Rough Anthology
Billionaire Rock
Billionaire Rock - part 2

Dominating PA Series
Her Personal Assistant - Part 1
Her Personal Assistant - Part 2
Her Personal Assistant - Part 3
Her Personal Assistant Box Set

Firehouse Romance Series
Caught in Flames
Burning With Desire
Craving the Heat
Firehouse Romance Complete Collection

Fortune Riders MC Series
Billionaire Biker
Billionaire Ransom
Billionaire Misery

Hades' Spawn Motorcycle Club
One You Can't Forget
One That Got Away

One That Came Back
One You Never Leave
Hades' Spawn MC Complete Series

Heart of the Battle Series
Celtic Viking
Celtic Rune
Celtic Mann
Heart of the Battle Series Box Set

Justice Series
Seeking Justice
Finding Justice
Chasing Justice
Pursuing Justice
Justice - Complete Series

Love You Series
Love Life: Billionaire Dance School Hot Romance
Need Love
My Love

Managing the Bosses Series
The Boss
The Boss Too
Who's the Boss Now
Love the Boss
I Do the Boss
Wife to the Boss
Employed by the Boss
Brother to the Boss
Senior Advisor to the Boss
Forever the Boss
Gift for the Boss - Novella 3.5

Christmas With the Boss

Moment in Time
Highlander's Bride
Victorian Bride
Modern Day Bride
A Royal Bride
Forever the Bride

R&S Rich and Single Series
Alex Reid
Parker

Saving Forever
Saving Forever - Part 1
Saving Forever - Part 2
Saving Forever - Part 3
Saving Forever - Part 4
Saving Forever - Part 5
Saving Forever - Part 6
Saving Forever Part 7
Saving Forever - Part 8

Southern Romance Series
Little Love Affair
Siege of the Heart
Freedom Forever
Soldier's Fortune

Tattooist Series
Confession of a Tattooist
Surrender of a Tattooist
Heart of a Tattooist

Tennessee Romance

Whisky Lullaby
Whisky Melody
Whisky Harmony

The Debt
The Debt: Part 1 - Damn Horse
The Debt: Complete Collection

The University of Gatica Series
The Recruiting Trip
Faster
Higher
Stronger
Dominate
No Rush

T.N.T. Series
Troubled Nate Thomas - Part 1
Troubled Nate Thomas - Part 2
Troubled Nate Thomas

Undercover Series
Perfect For Me
Perfect For You
Perfect For Us

Unknown Identity Series
Unknown
Unexposed
Unpublished

Standalone
Wash
Loving Charity
Summer Lovin'

Christmas Magic: A Romance Anthology
Love & College
Billionaire Heart
First Love
Frisky and Fun Romance Box Collection
Managing the Bosses Box Set #1-3